T0078004

THE
LAST ROYAL
MESSENGER

THE
LAST ROYAL
MESSENGER

GEORGE SULLIVAN

To order additional copies of this book, contact:
Xlibris
1-888-795-4274
www.Xlibris.com
Orders@Xlibris.com
810654

1

The cool morning air flowed through the window ruffling the curtains as it passed. Its presence graced Lady Carmen leaving goose bumps across her bare skin. She shivered then huddled under the covers that had been pushed back midway the bed sometime in the night. A cock began its morning call and shortly after a banging sound could be heard. A hammer banging a stubborn nail into rough bark. Lady Carmen turned over on her side, moaned and tried to cover her ears with her pillow.

She could smell the smoke of a freshly lit hearth and knew that breakfast would be announced soon. It all seem too early for this, was the night really that short, or did she spend too much of it away.

The bedroom door slammed open and Lord John's deep intake of breath and loud footfalls moving across the wood plank floors was heard before he snatched back the curtains allowing the cool breeze and dawn's faint light fully into the room. "Tis a lovely morning, wouldn't you say?"

He seen his wife twist and turn away from the window. He walked over to the end of the bed and roughly patted its end. "My lovely wife it is time to rise and prepare for the morning meal. Come now, we have a very busy day ahead of us."

Lady Carmen moaned then snatched the covers from over her head when Lord John sat heavily on the bed and bounced a few times. "What is the meaning of this, John? And get your oafish self off of the bed."

"Ah! I do truly love you too. But the meaning of this beautiful and oh so merry morning, is that our son may become a prince soon."

"You silly man, in order for our Caleb to become a prince; he has to marry a princess." she sat up wiping her eyes and yawned.

"Ah, yes precisely". Lord John said. He took the rolled up parchment from out of his inside pocket and handed it to his wife.

"What is that?"

"An invitation and hopefully a possibility. Here, read it."

She took it from his strong yet neatly cared for hands and unraveled it. Quickly she read its contents as her eyes widen, her breath caught then she read it again slowly. An excited screech escaped her and she tried to scramble out of bed. "Could this be true John?"

"Indeed it is." he answered her with a wide smile "The king has thought of our Caleb as a suitor for the princess."

"Oh my lord! Yes, what a lovely morn it is." She beamed a big beautiful smile as Lord John watched her scurry about mumbling something to herself. Suddenly she stopped and turned to her husband. "Have you told Caleb yet?"

"No I have not." he said getting up from the bed. "I thought to do so at the morn's meal. I know that you wish to be there. So let's get a move on. I will send in your maid servant to help you prepare." Lord John walked to the door. "We must send a response to the king. I know your clothing fit will last a while as well, so the sooner you come down, the sooner you can have at it. I only ask that you do not have either of us too stiff to be comfortable."

Lady Carmen scoffed at him holding her hand to her breast. "Yes I love you to my fair lady". Lord John said after she warned him off. He left the bedroom and sent in her maid servant.

When Caleb came to the table and sat, he grabbed his glass of orange juice then looked about the table. No one was absent but something definitely was not right. He took a gulp from his glass then cleared his throat. "Ahem. Ah father is there something that I missed? Has someone passed?"

"Now Caleb, why would you say something like that?" his father said sounding surprised.

"Then why is everyone so quiet? And why is mother looking at me like that?"

Lord John looked at his wife then back to his son. "What do you mean?"

"You know what I mean. Like she is holding something back. She looks like she is ready to burst. What's going on?"

Lord John took a deep breath and spook. "Well, the king has decided that it is time for the princess to get married."

Caleb's brow wrinkled, he looked from his father to his mother then back to his father. Yet said nothing, but waited for his father to continue.

"Well the king believes that if we have not decided on a bride for you, ahem...;" he cleared his throat upon seeing Caleb's brow crinkle further and his face tighten. "...that you would be a suitable choice among the invited suitors." he finished.

"Oh Caleb, isn't that great?" his mother beamed.

Caleb looked at both his parents then the servants waiting about them. "Will you please excuse us?" he asked the servants, who looked to Lord John.

"Yes, it I s okay; go on." he told them. When they left the dining hall Lord John sat up straighter in his chair. "My son..." he began but was cut off.

"How many suitors does she have, and why me?"

"There is five in all. Lord Jeffery's boy, Brain. Lord Gregory's son, Gregory the third. The king has mentioned of two princes, one from the west. I believe it will be the Pikes. They are looking to close the connection between our kingdoms. And the Fontz, one of their boys."

"Why now?"

"Well it is clear that our queen will not bare another child. The king has only two daughter sand he wants an heir. Someone dependable, someone that will be good for our kingdom and his daughter."

"So, father how is it that I have been chosen as a suitor? Everyone knows that I do not favor the princess."

"Oh, Caleb don't say that." Lady Carmen said. "You two would make such a beautiful pair."

"No we would not."

"But you would be a prince, and heir to the throne."

Caleb looked pleadingly at his father. "Father?"

"I think the king is looking out for the best interest of the kingdom. He knows that you, our family is among the highest of his backings when it comes to the kingdom and his decisions. You have fought valiantly beside him in two wars, you put the kingdom first, you know politics, and you are a good man."

"But father, he too knows that I do not favor the princess. Why would he consider me? Gregory and Brian both fought at his side as well as I and they both fancy the Princess Elizabeth."

"Caleb, our family is closest to the king's family. We are also an old family among the nobles. It would be a slight not to consider us, you among the choices. And I believe that the king believes, Caleb; that you would do your duties to the kingdom first. As do we." Lord John said looking from Caleb to his wife, then back to Caleb. Caleb's face showed that he did not like the way this was turning out.

"Caleb, we would be so grateful to accept the king's invitation." Lady Carmen said.

"Nothing is final, my boy." Lord John told him.

"But Caleb you would be the next king." lady Carmen told him.

"Yes, but an unhappy one." Caleb said then got up from the table.

Both of his parents sat quietly for a while. Lady Carmen broke the silence. "What is wrong with that boy John, he should be happy the king thought of him."

"Yes he should. But we both also know that he is right. The boy would be unhappy. The princess does not favor Caleb either."

"Huh, that is absurd. Why would she not favor our Caleb? He is handsome, strong, good in politics, and he comes from a good old family."

"Yes, but he is not self-centered, ruthless and conniving as our princess is. He would try to be too just and by the rules while the Princess Elizabeth may desire the opposite. They would be in each other's way." Again they sat in silence until Lord John said, "We will accept this invitation. Make our appearance as expected. But I will have to speak to the king about our son as his first choice on his list." his shook his head in confusion, "the king does know that our children do not favor each other." Then he too got up from the table and walked off.

Lady Carmen's mood was not truly spoiled. She picked up her glass and clanged it with her fork. The servants returned to the dining hall. "Clear away this stuff, we are finished here." the servants nodded and began to clear the table. Lady Carmen sat a few moments longer then departed herself. Yes, they will accept the king's invitation and they will make a grand and beautiful appearance, one fit for their name and station.

All the preparation would be left up to her. She decided that she would not be so gloomy. She would make the necessary preparations and enjoy it for them all.

Time was passing and all the intended suitors (the ladies of the house) made their preparations to attend the king's invitation. There was to be a tourney, small challenges among the suitors and parties for mingling. Three days, this will last, then a choice will be made. The princess will have a husband prince who will be named heir to the throne. The kingdom and its surroundings were in a blissful buzz. Lady Carmen had her own confidants among the castle and waited to learn the order of arrival for the intended suitors. She had planned to be last, or next to it. Their family's arrival would be grand and fit for their future king.

The men, Lord John, and her son Caleb had left all the preparations to her. Of all three of their children, Caleb was the only one she had to prepare for. Mary, their daughter and second child was a playmate to the king's second child. Harry, he was away in one of Lord John's brother's care as a squire and would attend with him.

Lady Carmen ordered all the fabric for their clothing and her knowing their sizes already set to work with the tailors and seamstress. She had the men's tourney amour polished, the family banner ready, a gift ordered for the king and queen and both the princesses. Their horses and carriage was readied and all who would accompany their procession. She awaited news from her confidants and upon its deliverance was quick in her assessments. Everyone knew her son's valiancy and prowess to be a tough opponent in politics and a vicious fighter on the field. They knew as well the king favored him above all the other intended. Lady Carmen would make sure that her son had a grand entrance.

Lord John knew that Caleb did not like the prospect of joining with the princess at all, but he knew that as he watched his son these last few weeks, he would do his duty to the king and kingdom first. Caleb would not dishonor their family either. For his son's sake he wished the king had choose someone else to favor.

2

Princess Elizabeth could not understand to save her life why her mother and sister were so happy this morning. They acted as if they were the one getting 'auctioned' off; no she meant engaged. If they thought that they were getting rid of her, they were wrong. Her father had already made it clear that the 'lucky' man would be staying here with her. Her fiance would become a crowned prince and heir to their kingdom and throne. A throne that should be hers. She had argued a plenty that she could rule the kingdom after her father better than any man her father thought to attach to her. She was his heir and should be crowned. His retort was that rulership belonged to a man. There was never a princess as heir and it wasn't his right to change tradition. His last words were always 'no-one wants to be ruled by a women, look at how you acting'. She pleaded with her mother to interject on her behalf, but she never would. A woman has her place and it is not at the head of a kingdom, she would say. None of which the princess wanted to hear.

So after many failed attempts to be declared the rightful heir, she decided that she would have her say in who would or should be her suitor. And there again she failed. But she was not upset to learn of her four intended suitors. She knew all of them and knew she could bully and or seduce them into allowing her ultimate rule. But there was one last suitor that was not revealed to her. Everyone claimed that they had no knowledge as to who it was. The king told no-one of his choice. However, this morning she knew that her mother and sister knew, they found out and were delighted in the king's choice.

This would be the day that she would discover the fifth suitor, and three days later she would be engaged with hopes of her own reign; or so she thought.

She could not find a single quiet spot in the whole castle. People were happier at the thought of getting a male heir for the king then they were that she was getting engaged. It was supposed to be an event for her but turned out to be something else for her father. She wished that she could run away and leave it all behind, leave it to her father and soon to be heir. But she knew that she would not make it far. But, the thought was still appealing. She allowed herself to be whisked along, dressed and made. Her mother would not put up with her moping and dragging about.

Her first suitor and his entourage had arrived and her mother yelped with delight, hustled them along to find the king. They were all to be pleasant, cheerful, and delighted to welcome their guess into their humble home. Even though she was not truly happy, she had to admit that she did look beautiful and what she had seen of the preparations thus far, was splendid. Her mother had done a very good job for this occasion.

Her father came to meet them and he was looking grand. He was the ideal king. Tall, broad of shoulders, thick in the chest, strong and very handsome. And on top of all of this, his authority was sound and obeyed to the fullest letter (whether people liked it or not). His smile beamed bright as his three beautiful ladies came to meet him. He held out his hands wide to receive the queen first, placing a kiss on each side of her face. His daughters were next, Elizabeth first then Susan. He stepped back looking at the three of them.

"My beautiful ladies, our first guest has arrived. Let us be gracious host and go greet them, shall we." He offered his arm to the queen who readily accepted it. They led the way as the princesses followed, with all their maidens and servants behind them; the king's and queen's council along with advisers in tow. Their own greeting procession was not small.

They marched their way down hallways, out the front entrance to the castle and stood before the draw bridge. Their wait lasted only a few minutes until they saw the black banner with the huge bear upon it. The Fontz had arrived first. It had been a while since Francis had paid them a visit. He was very handsome but Elizabeth knew that he was not very much into politics and fancied all the ladies. If he was to become king, there would be a lot of bastard children running around. Tall, dark and handsome, sweet with words, he was irresistible among the ladies. She could rule the kingdom with him as a front. She smiled to herself at he thought. She felt a hand tighten on her arm and looked to see her mother smiling at her and she smiled back. (Only if she knew what I was smiling about, she would frown Elizabeth thought). Frederick was too young to be considered so she did not worry about him.

The king and queen of Chamell, their carriage was high and just as black as their banner. Six Clydesdale pulled them along and now pranced among the two other carriages that accompanied them. Ten other singled riders were at their sides and back. A guard of thirteen in all. Elizabeth considered that they brought a few of their own ladies in waiting the queen and other servants for the princes and the king. Maybe thirty in all. A respectful company for a visiting king.

Before their horses hooves touched the bridge they stopped. The guards dismounted and the carriage doors were opened. The queen and king stepped out of carriage and the sons followed. When they all stood together, they bowed and curtsied across the bridge to their host. Their arrival was loudly announced then the king returned their bows. He opened his arms wide and welcomed them to come. The bridge was no small walk, so they re-entered their carriage and their horses carried them across the bridge to their host.

One after the other, the intended came, were welcomed and showed their place for their temporary tenure.

Lord Gregory was next barring the king's banner first. A crowned griffon ascending the sky on a blue banner. Lord Gregory's own was a mountain lion perched on a cliff looking down. Their procession was fifteen people in all. Lord Gregory's son Gregory the third fancied Elizabeth very much and pressed his parents to visit every chance they could. Upon several council meetings on which Lord Gregory sat, he brought his son with him. Ever since the princess could remember she had bullied Gregory into doing whatever she wanted him to do. All she had to do was ask and he would happily do her bidding. And nothing has changed throughout the time in them knowing each other. The princess knew that if he became king, he would be faithful and only a face as well. She could still rule if she married him.

Lord Jeffery came next. He too bore the king's banner first then his own. His was a huge fist holding a war hammer, red was the banner's color. Since Lord Jeffery's wife had passed away, he ahd not remarried. His niece had come to stay with them and accepted the role as lady of the house. She would hold that position until the lord married again or his son took over in his stead. This day she did not accompany them. Lord Jeffery's procession was twelve.

Princess Elizabeth remembered young Brian and herself had tried to run off twice. She was besotted with him, she told her parents that she would marry him and no-one else. She had kissed him several times and had made plenty of promises. Brian, who was a bold presence to others was always shy and submissive to her. Always was he the strong, bold, yet well-spoken gentleman. In stature brain was almost a match to her father. There was none other comparable to him and only one who she knew that cold best him. Someone who was almost a spitting image of her father. Someone she loathed and did not wish to think of at the moment. She shivered at a thought then continued to watch Brain.

The next to arrive was the Pikes. This, Elizabeth could not understand in her father's choice; King and Queen Bestle's son Conrad as one of her intended. These people, the princess thought were close to being considered barbaric. They had a structural regime, but it was far from civilized. They were heavy into slavery and paraded their dying adversary along on spikes until they died. They were strong on the battlefield but like lifeless rocks when it came to politics. And King Bestle boasted of concubines and plenty of bastard children. Conrad, strong and handsome, but dumb would be no different than the rest of his people.

Their banner was a misty gray with a well-muscled, vicious looking dog ready to attack on it. She believed the black and brown dog was called a wielder. The eldest daughter accompanied them so that she, who was of age to marry could see how it was done, to choose a husband. Princess Elizabeth envied her that she could choose who she wished to marry or at least be a candidate for marriage. All the land west of them, savage they may be; gave their daughters a choice to pick who would compete for their hand. They all hoped for the most brutish.

Their procession was fifty strong and only seven of which were female. The princess also heard that their arrival was part by ship, they left behind twenty others to guard it. She had thought this to be quite big, but her father dismissed it saying that he was surprised that they arrived in so small a number.

Their spicy food and horse breeding is what interested her father and they were more than ready to trade, to build better ties. Her father's land was known for its plentiful and fast growing trees. They were well known for the ships they built and the navy force they kept. A protection that the Pikes needed. They were surrounded by water on three sides and had no short list of adversaries who wanted their land and horses. There were also large fowl that inhabited the only their lands. They too were very popular and good meat if cooked right.

Well now, all that she knew had arrived and were properly greeted, showed to their quarters for their stay and were now preparing for the noon day meal. The castle was abuzz and all were on their best behavior. While Princess Elizabeth continuously let her gaze brows the crowd, she notice that her father had frequently vanished from their group and upon following him twice had discovered that he was standing alone at the draw bridge looking out. She assume that he was looking for the last intended. She let it be and decided to let him worry about that.

At the luncheon King Charles appeared to be enjoying himself and joined in with some of the conversations. The queen, however, noticed that it was not wholeheartedly. He ate well but hardly touched his drink. He glanced at the door more often than not and seemed to be listening out for something. Whatever he was waiting for was bugging him and started to show. Queen Alicene tried to act like she didn't know what it was, but she was more than certain that if asked she would answer true. Lord John's procession had not arrived as yet and there was no sign of them. When the king had confided in her on his choice of Caleb, she could tell that something about that choice had bothered him. Now it showed partly in their response. It was two words written plainly, 'We accept'. It was plain enough that it was not a happy response and that it was most likely done out of respect for the king. All knew that Caleb could not tolerate the princess to long and she loath him. No-one knew the reason why but it had always been that way between those two. She now had hoped that they had no changed their minds or could not convince Caleb to agree. The queen knew that the king and Caleb were close and favored each other in mind, but it was more than that; Caleb had actually looked a spitting image of the King. They were alike in every way. She had thought back to the many whispered rumor as a young Caleb began to grow and mature how much he resembled the king, more than his own father, Lord John. Had the king and Lady Carmen been unfaithful? They had both swore their innocence, but it did not dispelled the rumors. It was not until a sorcerer was brought in to check the truth of their words through magic, only then had the rumors stop.

Lunch had ended and upon the king's allowance, the queen had ushered the group through the many gardens as they spoke and sipped wine. The king was quiet throughout.

It was two hours after the lunch that there was a loud uproar. Horns blared and people rushed about. The last of the intended had finally arrived and King Charles rushed off with concern on his face. Queen Alicene had excused them and she and the princesses trailed off after the king. They rushed up with him as Princess Elizabeth pleaded to know who it was that arrived, who was the last intended. It seemed that on-one paid her any mind as they reached their spot and waited for the rest of their meeting group to arrive behind them.

The king's banner could be seen held high. Foot steps thundered the ground in unison and a gold banner with black trim came into view. A night clad in black armor sat up atop a bastion stallion with sword drawn. The banner of Lord John Clemons of Brownsin arrived accompanied with two black carriages. Fifteen riding guards and twenty five foot soldiers and in between them another two wagons covered in black drapes could be seen. King Charles and Queen Alicene beamed with smiles and stood tall waiting to accept their favorite guest. Princess Elizabeth stood still with a blank expression on her face. The young lady Mary fidgeted fighting back the urge to run out to meet her family.

The riders dismounted and with the foot soldiers approached the draw bridge. They parted leaving a path between them, two sides of forty men. The driver opened the carriage door and out stepped Lord John and Lady Carmen. The second carriage was door was opened and out stepped Caleb, looking as much the intended prince he was to be. He joined with his parents and the soldiers bent the knee to them first, then turned clasped their fist upon their breast and bowed to the king. Lord John, Lady Carmen and Caleb walked between the soldiers and stood at the edge of the draw bridge and bowed to their king and queen. Their names were announced loudly, then they stood.

King Charles had squeezed his wife's hand, turning to her he smiled all of his approval. There was no trace of worriation or disappointment about him now. However, Princess Elizabeth looked like she was ready to sulk off and throw a fit. There was no way that Caleb could be her fifth intended. She silently begged for it not to be so. But the king opened his arms to accept them and they, instead of getting back into their carriages; walked the length of the bridge to their king.

Lord John had apologized for their late arrival and added that he thought that the king would want to spend some time with the foreign kings and queens, so they thought to hold back on their arrival. The king asked about the other two wagons and was told that they were gifts to be presented later. The king accepted this and led them inside. The young Lady Mary marched happily beside her brother smiling and holding his hand. Princess Elizabeth gave a tight smile and walked quietly on the other side of Caleb. Neither spoke to the other after their greeting.

3

All the guest were gathered together in the gardens where the king, queen and the princess fluttered among each group. The intended, all at least knew of each other and everyone appeared to be enjoying themselves. They were given reprieve for personal time among themselves at which time Lord John did not hesitate to seek out a private conversation with the King. When they were out of hearing distance, Lord John spoke first.

"My king, my old friend, why do you torture our children so?"

"I know John." the king said dropping the tension from his shoulders. "But I have no choice." he turned to face John. "But ask yourself, without personal emotion. Who would you rather see sit the throne?" he did not give Lord John a chance to answer. "I did that, John, I asked myself who would be best for the kingdom, who knows our history, who fights for us who would treat our people and foreign neighbors fairly, who could keep authority out of the hands of my emotionally spoiled daughter? There are many who look the part, I seriously considered Prince Conrad. He is head strong and stubborn like a bull, but to our politics… dumb just the same. My daughter could manipulate just about any suitor I suggest, one way or the other. But we both know that is not the case with Caleb.

"But they can't stand each other Charles."

"I know."

"Would you like to see your kingdom divided?" King Charles walked away. "That's what would happen." Lord John spoke up.

"John," King Charles turned back to him "I know how my daughter is. But, do you think that she would go that far?"

Lord John walked up to the king and took his arm, they continued to walk. "You know Elizabeth wants to rule, solely." The king nodded his agreement. "Have you ever stopped to think that she may have already started to rally her own people, spies and confident, family to her side." he paused "Sympathizers. Elizabeth is very smart, she get that from you. But she is also her mother's child and coming fast into her own womanhood. You, and I have been married for some time now. We know our wives have their ways of doing things."

Yes, I know what you mean." King Charles smiled at that thought. "I guess we can't put it past our daughters. The things that our wives do."

"Or try to do." Lord John added.

"Okay but John, why do you think our children act so toward each other?"

"That I could never figure out."

"Have they ever done anything outright harmful to one another? Besides the little challenging remarks and battle of wits? Have either openly declared that they hated each other?"

"No."

"What have they done other than act like a male and female child towards each other with something to prove. John, since our children reached that age that they think the opposite gender is icky, where girls are silly and boys are stupid. Caleb and Elizabeth have not outgrown their childish thoughts of each other."

"What are you saying, Charles?"

"I'm saying that it is time that they start acting like adults and not petty children. They are compatible John, and you know it to be true."

They stood there looking at each other. Lord John did not want to see it the king's way but he had no argument against him. Charles knew he had him cornered, he raised his eyebrows and opened his arms open in challenge. Lord John shook his head, "As much as I think it would pain Caleb, I see no reason to disagree with you." Lord John looked up in certainty. "I will not be the one to tell him any of this though."

King Charles laughed, "And neither will I. We will let things play out their own course. If we both know Caleb, he will not shun a challenge just because of Elizabeth's feelings. He will do his best and win, that we know."

"We will see how events turn out on the morrow."

"Yes we will." King Charles said patting Lord John on the back. "So my Dear John..." King Charles began as they headed back. "...what is in those other wagons that you brought?"

"Ah my king, would you force me to break a promise to the lady of my house?"

"Oh no!" King Charles said seriously, then laughed. I would not bring that wrath upon you." they both laugh and continued small talk on their way.

At the same time that Lord John sought out the king, Princess Elizabeth had branched off and quietly followed Caleb. She had taken off her shoes and gathered up her dress from dragging on the ground. Caleb had walked alone with his head down not looking for or seeking out any company. He walked down several halls turning here and there and finally came to a halt at a junction not far from a window with a bench under it. He sat down fiddling with the bottom of his coat, lost in thought. Elizabeth had eased up on him and slapped him on the back of the neck. He jumped up, "What in the..."

"Hush up you dope." she cut him off, then stepped up to him poking him in the chest. "What are you doing here?"

"Well I..."

"You know what I mean, so don't act stupid."

"Well I didn't send myself an invitation."

"Are you trying to ruin me?"

"I have..."

"I knew it was too good to be true. Then you showed up."

"I..."

She scoffed at him, "Looking and acting all princely. What's the meaning of this charade?"

"Well, are you going to let me talk?" Caleb finally got out.

"Hmph. You need to return home."

"I can't just leave."

"Well then, get sick. Say you have the flu."

"Then the King will just postpone the tourney."

"Well then, well then, ugh." Elizabeth said in frustration. "Jump out of that window there." she said pointing at the window Caleb sat under.

"Elizabeth are you mad? As much as it does not please me to leave, I would rather see you live in tournament at my presence than commit suicide. I am not that desperate."

"Ugh, I can't stand you." she tried to slap him but he stepped away.

"The feeling is the same."

"Why did your father have to accept the invitation?"

"Why did your father have to send one?"

Elizabeth walked away from him folding her arms about herself. "There has to be a way out of this mess our parents put us in. Ugh, I can't believe they would do this to me."

"You are not the only one unhappy here. I did not ask for any of this either."

Elizabeth turn to him suddenly. "You have to lose." she said.

"What?"

"You have to lose the tourney."

"I cannot do that." Caleb said shaking his head.

"Yes you can, you must." she said walking up to him.

"Elizabeth I would be disgracing my family, and the king. Everyone knows that I am one of the best, if not the best at archery, dueling, wrestling, hand-to hand combat. I have been trained in battle since I could walk and history and politics since I could talk. I cannot purposely lose." They were quiet for a moment then Caleb said, "It is up to you."

"Me?"

"Yes you."

"But I..."

"You have to prove to your father that I am not the right man for you. Come up with something that the others can do better than me. Do something, improvise the contest."

She almost stepped up to him and hugged him but caught herself. "You may be smarter than you look." she gathered up her dress and hurried off, "But you're still a stupid boy." she called back.

"It was my idea, so I'm smarter than you." he called out.

Elizabeth stopped a minute, turned and stuck out her tongue at him then ran off.

"And she calls me stupid, silly girl." Caleb said to himself.

Later that evening when dinner had commenced and all were gathered in the huge hall, the king thanked everyone for coming, blessed their meeting and eating then dinner was served. Fowl, ham deer, a multitude of sea food, sweet potatoes, mashed potatoes, rice and noodles, an assortment of sauces and a variety of vegetables. String beans, peas, and turn-ups, greens and lettuce. They had sweet bread and rolls, buttered biscuits and onion bread, four different wines graced the table and a new campaign from the east-mountains. All were dressed fabulously and looked the part of royalty. But by desert time, belts, girdles, and tongues were loose. The king gave in and called for a reprieve to ease their bottoms and have some song and dance. And that they did. They danced and drank well into the night.

Lord John had disappeared briefly then when he returned, he called for everyone's attention. He praised the king and queen and their beautiful daughters and with a wave of the hand, the doors to the hall were opened wide. Lord John's men pulled and pushed into the center of the room the two wagons he brought with him. He pointed to the wagons and continued his talk.

"A present for the royal family. For years of friendship, it has been known how much the king and queen loved their visit to the mid-eastern mountain lands of Shekstan. Their intrigue of wild and foreign cats was the high light of their talk." The queen's eyes were as wide as her smile. "From my humble family to yours, my king we present you with these gifts."

The first wagon was uncovered and revealed two white and black striped cubs. The king and queen rushed forward, "Open the cage." the king announced, "So that we may graciously accept our gifts." Tears of surprise and joy teased the queen's eyes as the little cubs were placed in her arms. The audience loudly applauded. With the uproar of noise another sound was faintly heard. Everyone looked around and quieted down.

"Well, since that gift has revealed itself. I will move on to it next." he turned to his wife "My wife's idea that I cannot take credit for. But to the lovely Princess Susan, a much talked about wish, my family presents this to you." and the other half of the wagon was revealed. The beautiful multi-colored birds screeched and flapped their wings. Princess Susan's hands shot to her mouth as she suppressed a scream. "The Native Crest birds of Chinlag." Lord John said.

Lady Carmen was closest, so it was to her that Princess Susan ran and hugged. She then went to Lord John, curtsied and thanked him. She walked around the cage holding them and asked if she could hold one. There was placed a string around the foot of the bird then a gauntlet on the princess' arm before the bird was handed to her.

The attention was brought back to Lord John, "Last but not at all the least, to our Princess Elizabeth; another gift that I cannot take credit for. But thanks to my Caleb and his observation and memory, we present this gift to you." All turned to the last wagon that was just as big as the first. The curtain was pulled back to reveal a huge tank filled with all kinds of multi-colored fish.

Princess Elizabeth was suspicious at first on hearing Caleb's name. But upon seeing the beautiful creatures she could no longer suppression her pleasure. She eased her way toward the tank, stopped and curtsied to Lord John and he slightly bowed in return. Her eyes looked for Caleb and upon seeing him she nodded her head. He returned the nod and gestured to the tank. She walked around the tank amazed, naming all the fish she could. Most of which she only seen in books.

Conversation picked back up, music again played but softly and the audience filled with laughter at the clumsy yet energetic cubs as they pranced, rolled, and stumbled about legs and scrambling feet the night was filled with gaiety. Everyone was comfortable and at ease as the night went on.

A servant came up to the king and whispered something in his ear. The king nodded and the servant walked hastingly to the door and let another guest in. In walked Jared with a letter in his hand straight to the king.

The intake of breath then silence was shocking, even the music had stopped. The cubs looked around in confusing and the birds screeched. Jared reached the king and bowed to his knee, upon standing he kissed the king's extended hand then handed him the letter. But before the king opens it, he bids everyone to carry on in their merriment. The king walks off while Jared follows and waits. King Charles read the letter twice and wipes a tear from his eyes. He and Jared speak briefly then Jared hands him an ink well and quill that he keeps on his person. The king subscribes a small message at the end of the letter then hands it back to Jared. Jared takes it, bows and turns to walk away but the king calls him back. He embraces Jared tightly then held him at arms-length. King Charles takes a ring off his finger and places it on Jared's hand, then Jared exits the hall just as he entered.

4

The shock and silence filled the hall upon seeing the Royal Messenger. What was he doing here? Did the king send for him, or did he have a message for the king? He was the Royal Messenger, answerable to no-one but the king. No even the queen had a right to question him. Jared's presence loomed heavy in the minds of the attendants. He was quiet and mysterious, and everyone knew he was deadly. Trained from birth to be so. For him to be here, something had to going on.

Queen Alicene was suspicious of Jared because he and the king made it clear that he answered only to the king. It has always been that way with the royal messengers. No matter how she tried to bribe or persuade him, Jared never gave in to her womanly ways. So the queen too, like everyone else was shocked to see him. She begrudge herself for stumbling about. Quickly bringing herself to her senses she eased off from the crowd and spoke to one of her servants. The king was not the only one to have messengers around the castle. Although his were the only official ones. Her conversation was brief and she came right back to the crowd as if she never left. She must know what the king is up to.

However, Queen Alicene was not the only one to take advantage of the slight distraction of such a demanding presence. All the other ladies rushed to their husbands pretending to dance as they spoke about the surprise visit of the messenger. Many people had thought that there were no more, and with the use of magic now; an easier way to send and receive messages. The station of a Royal Messenger should have been closed. No more men were being trained and Jared was the last one left, and alive. One would be surprised at how much a royal messenger was sought, how they were besieged on all sides upon their journey and more frequently than not, they were killed just to learn their message.

King Charles was the only one to hold on to his last royal messenger when magic was decided to be used. But he had his own reasons for keeping Jared at his side, and he was telling no-one, not even Jared himself.

As Princess Elizabeth stood back and watched all the nobles and the two visiting kings and queens mumble to themselves in huddled groups, she noticed quite a bit of servants being summoned then run off before their presence was clearly marked. Many rushed in and out before the royal messenger took his own leave. The princess was more shocked at the reaction of the people towards the royal messenger then Jared himself. She had never feared Jared and learned most of her politics from him, although in secret. More than any man she ever met, she had crush on him for a very long time. She was attracted to his mysteriousness, to the thought of how dangerous he was and how his presence brought about more silence faster than the king himself. Jared did not know his own background and when she asked her father about it she was sternly admonished not to question about him, his background, family, or his coming and going. The king had forbid her to see him for years, then without notice he lifted it. Never had she seen such a reaction as this and never had she seen Jared dressed so. She tore her eyes away from the whispering nobles to appraise Jared. Dressed almost completely in all black, his shirt cuffs and collar hinted a dark gray. He wore a cape the color of drying blood and his long black hair that he wore loose and hanging was now braided tightly with a silver ball tied at its end. His hands were adorned with several rings. A short sword hung from one side of his waist and a set of black daggers from the other side. His long sword was strapped across his back. His attention was for no-one but the king. Jared was the only one allowed in the presence of the king armed so at any giving time, besides the king's personal body guard. The princess knew that some of those rings were magical as was his long sword enchanted to be unbreakable. She also knew that even though she had never seen Jared dressed for his role as Royal Messenger, Jared had more weapons about him. There was no question about that, he was definitely going on a mission; one that was unexpected by all in the room. It used to excite her to dream about what the journey and adventure of a royal messenger would be like. She had let pass all the parts about them being hunted down and killed. Their missions being intercepted by spies of foreign kingdoms and envious home nobles that were partial to the king. As she judge this night's reaction to Jared and the hurried disappearance of servants, the reality of his role and the danger to became real to her. Now she feared for her friend's life. Princess knew that the rest of the night would be pretend just for the king's sake. She too, like everyone else wanted to know what the Royal Messenger's visit was about. Knowing that when this party was over, the night would be far from it.

Lady Chelsey, daughter of Lord Wilford and Lady Patrice, wife of Lord Gregory fidgeted in her husband's arms as they danced. He tried to calm her, reassure her that all was well. But she would not listen. It was the way Jared looked their way upon exiting the hall and now the king occasionally stared at them. Lord Gregory and Lady Chelsey were among the king's backers, but they were in agreement with their parents to banish princess Georgette. They knew the truth along with two other older noble's families.

When Charles became king and a few years late Jared was brought to him as infant, they were in agreement to have the child killed. The king forbid and threatened to wipe out the whole family of any who attempted, noble or not. The most that was achieved among the knowing nobles was to have any knowledge about his background silence and kept hidden. Not even Jared was to know.

Jared's whole existence was a burden to them and know from the looks of these two men, Lady Chelsey was sure that the secret would be no more. Their credibility and standing with the king might be tarnished in the near future. The people of the kingdom and the council would be furious to learn what the nobles had done at the command of King Charles's mother, Queen Juliah. Lady Chelsey swore to her husband that she seen more of the sky blue letters tucked in Jared's waist when he turned from the King. The letters, if he read them all; most likely told him the truth. She was sure that the looks Jared gave her told it all. They would soon be doomed.

Much later that night Caleb tossed in his bed his mind would not let him rest. Over and over in he dreamed that he was falling into a bottomless pit. Many were the hands that pushed him in.

He sat straight up throwing the covers off himself. He was drenched in sweat. This last dream was the worst of them all. Again many hands had pushed him, but as he looked at himself fall he seen that that he wore the outfit of a royal messenger. His thoughts pushed forth the night's party and the reactions towards his friend and part-time trainer. Jared had done something that made the whole hall fear him. But Caleb could not figure out what it was that had them in such a state. The only thing that came to mind was the way that Jared was dressed tonight. Everyone knew his role, but Caleb never seen him dress to carry out his office. Most of the young lordling hadn't and Caleb was sure of that. He seen that even Princess Elizabeth was amazed at seeing Jared dressed so. That not really what worried Caleb, the look that passed between Lord Gregory and Jared was nothing friendly and Caleb had never seen him look at anyone with such seriousness. But there was more, all the servants that were whispered to and rushed on upon his arrival was something suspicious. Than the constant stares King Charles gave from time to time to the Beals. They too were not friendly.

Queen Alicene was antsy for the rest of the night as well. Caleb had not missed much of what happened when Jared came into the hall. He got up and eased into his night robe for he needed some air and thought to entertain a thought of waking his father. Caleb thought that Jared was in danger and not from anyone who was considered a known foe, but from those who they counted among friends.

It wasn't long after he left his room that he slowed. Caleb heard whispering in an aggressive manner coming from one of the windows. He made straight to the nearest door outside and didn't bother to put anything on his feet for he did not want to be heard. There were more than two people in a heated, yet hushed conversation. The voices were familiar for the first part. He knew that Lord Gregory and Lady Chelsey were there. As he eased on he heard the voices of the King and Queen of Chamell also. Of to the side were several servants, none of which attended the nights party. As he continued on something else caught his attention further in the garden. Feet. Bare feet stuck out from under a bush on the opposite side of the garden. The group moved on and so did the bare feet slowly behind them. Caleb wanted to know who those feet belonged to. He couldn't cross the garden without being seen so he retraced his steps and went back inside. He raced down the hall and around the corner, and passed the library and sitting room. Thankful that the width of the garden was not great and he could easily get to the other side within minutes. Although running all the way. This was one of the smaller gardens that separated joint wings of the westside guest chambers. He reached the other side and silently crept through the door and into the garden.

The night air had not begun to be chilled yet so he did not have to worry about his breath being seen. He hastily walked the way he see the feet go. He didn't have far to go because they hung back far enough from the group not to be discovered. As he approached you could tell it was a female that spied upon the group. A hand brushed long blond tresses away and he knew immediately that it was Princess Elizabeth. He shook his head not surprised but thought how to get her attention without startling her to much. He tore the bottom button of his robe and threw at her. She stiffened and he could tell that she held her breath and a cry at being caught. When she turned and saw who it was, Caleb wave at her and smiled she jerked her hand from her mouth and mouth something foul at him. Elizabeth turned to look at the group than back to Caleb and headed his way. She shoved him back the way he came.

"What are doing here?" She whispered in frustration. "She whispered in frustration.

"The same thing as you, spying. "Caleb replied

"I'm not spying."

"Yes you are, I've seen your feet inside those bushes over there and you were hiding and following them. Now why?"

She squinted her eyes at him a moment. "What were you doing out the bed and in the garden?"

"Why do you have to be so difficult?" he asked

Elizabeth placed her hand on her hips. "Tell me what you heard and I'll tell you what I heard."

Caleb had noticed a small device in her hand and recognize it right away it was a listening device form by sorceress. She could hear very well with that thing. He gave in and told her to come inside. Neither of them wanted to leave the group and miss the rest of there was to hear. But with the two of them about, the chances of getting caught were grater. They reluctantly went inside and decided to go to the library and talk. Safely inside Caleb wasted no time.

"I believe your mother and the rest of them are planning to have someone killed."

"Jared." Elizabeth whispered

"Jared, the Royal Messenger! How do you know? Why would they?" Caleb could not suppress his surprise.

"Hold on will you and hold it down. What else did you hear?"

"Something about a Georgette ruining their plans, should have been killed a long time ago. But that was all. No, no. Something about a threat to your father and how could someone, something. They were all upset and moving away." He shook his head but then I saw your feet and they moved on. When I saw your feet follow I decided to come up behind whoever it was."

"Stupid, you could have gotten us both caught."

"But I didn't." Caleb shot back. "So what did you hear and don't say nothing much. I've seen that listening thing in your hand."

"Huh you're so nosy I can't stand you."

"Yeah, yeah. Alright but what did you hear?"

"Well, this Georgette is a Princess and she knows Jared's background."

"Jared is Prince?"

"I don't know. But somehow they think that whoever this Princess is she's a threat to my father. Something about they should had never let Jared be sent here."

"Could Jared be the king's son and rightful heir?"

"No. That was already in question when it was rumored that you was his son."

"Such hateful people, how could they spread such a rumor?"

"Caleb I'm sorry to tell you but I thought you were my brother as well for a while." Elizabeth confessed.

"Elizabeth how could you..."

"Well Caleb you look just like him, and a little like Jared. Sorry. But tell me you never thought about that, not once?"

"No." Caleb said firmly but Elizabeth just looked at him. "I'm serious. I have always been proud of my parents and to think that I might be the king's son would mean that my mother was unfaithful to my father. That is not a good thought. My mother an adulteress. What that would say about your father?"

"I understand what you say Caleb, But he is the king and..."

"That makes Okay for him to take another man's wife?"

"I'm not..."

"But you are. My parents were already married way before I was born."

Elizabeth didn't think of it that way and it showed on her face. She felt bad for suggesting that about Caleb's mother. "I didn't mean like that Caleb. I was just saying..."

"That it would be okay that your husband and future king slept around, had concubines and mistresses."

"Well I..."

"Would defiantly use it against him. But were changing the subject Elizabeth. What else did you hear?"

She wanted badly to respond to that last statement but knew it would do her no good. This is why she had wished Caleb not to be a suitor. He knew her to well. She snapped out of her thought. "Francis plans to cheat at the tourney. Somehow, most likely with magic. Something about a deal between the Bestle's and our old nobles. I think they want a joint kingdom. If I marry Francis that's what they eventually plan on doing. But they must wait until my father passes because he is... and certain nobles won't agree to us joining. They will see it as ceding our rule. If it is revealed who this Princess Georgette really is, it may cause a civil war. King Perciville is backing Lord Gregory and all who side with him."

"They're going to send people to kill Jared so he won't find the Princess."

"I was thinking across those same lines."

"Elizabeth, I think your father knows that Lord Gregory, and the rest are up to something. He knows that they are going to try and stop him, I think that is why he gave him that ring."

"Did you see the way he was looking at Lady Chelsey?"

"Yeah. Something is not right. But what can we do about it, without making a big ruckus. We can't just leave and try to follow Jared."

"No, father would have a royal fit. Especially with the tourney tomorrow and all." they were silent for a while.

"Write him a letter." Caleb said.

"What?"

"Yes, you can write him a letter of what you heard. Act like you are giving him a hug and slip it in his pocket."

"But why me? You could tell him."

"No, it wouldn't be right. It would look bad for me."

"How is that?"

"I am a suitor. If I write about another of your suitors cheating and the deal with the Bestles, it would look like I'm trying to undermine the competition and I see Francis as a threat to my chances. It can't be me. But with all you heard and I mean all you heard, it would be different. Think of it, Elizabeth; the queen, your mother is involved." that made her shoulders slump. "You have no ill will against your mother or the other nobles. Your father would believe you more because you are not supposed to know about Jared or Princess Georgette."

"Okay ok I'll do it. But I have to figure out a way..."

"The truth, minus my part." Caleb said with raised eyebrows.

"Alright." she said and got up from her chair. "I can't be too tired come the morrow, and neither can you. You are expected to be in the tourney. As much as I wish you would fall off a cliff and disappear..." Caleb started to reply but Elizabeth held out her hand. "You need to be careful. You are everyone's greatest threat." with that she turned and headed out of the library.

A few minutes later Caleb walked out of the library door, looked around and headed in the opposite direction.

Tonight was full of secret meetings and spying. This was the third party he came across tonight. First, all of the intended met but Caleb. They plotted against him. The second was a larger group, some of the parents of the intended. He could not, like the princess and Caleb, hear the conversation of the queen and her party. This started out as a simple, yet innocent competition for a lady's hand and the prize of the throne at hand as well. He should have known better. King Charles slowly walked back to his bed chambers. With the morrow events would come a whole skin of nasty worms. Who else knows what else would come with it.

5

Jared had already prepared to leave before he went to the king and upon him leaving him he set out. The bundle of letters that he had with him were a great temptation and he though them to be a distraction to his mission. Before leaving he placed them in the king's chambers without reading one of them. He had a mission to find and bring to the king a lady that he once held dear to him. A lady that knew his own background. A lady that was on her dying bed and whose safety and life might be threatened by the king's own nobles. Jared was to protect this lady at all cost, even his own life if necessary. He had the authority of the king on his hand, but even the king thought that not enough and warned Jared to be careful and cautious of everyone. He had seen tears in the king's eyes and knew the letters to be of a serious nature. He would not fail to find this lady.

When he first received the letter and told to let no-one see it but the king, he was suspicious. No-one came to him anymore. Magic was the means to deliver messages now. But when the king set him on this mission he knew that magic could not be trusted. The king wanted no-one else to know what the letters were about. With magic, the message could be intercepted or spied on. But with a Royal Messenger nothing was useful. Something was done to them at a young age to prevent their minds from being tampered with. Their memories were exact and revealed only to the one they chose. Many council members and nobles found them to be nuisance because they could not get anything out of them and they answered to no-one but the king. They argued that it was not humane to train a child in such a way. For the training for a child, what they went through to become a Royal Messenger was near life threatening. But once they grew up and the training was complete, they were like killing predators and unpredictable. They were inhumane and took a life too easily without regard. The council and nobles had won out and no, more were trained. Since Jared was already in the process of training, to stop it would kill him. Therefore he was the last one trained. He thought it was no coincidence that shortly after the decree to stop training Royal Messengers, history reveals that they were suddenly dying off. The historians own thoughts were that they were being killed, just in case the decree was ever overturned. There would be none left to train more. The instructions on training a Royal Messenger were never wrote down and were locked in the memory of only the Royal messengers. So Jared was the last one of his kind and saved only by the king and his quick thinking to enhance whatever was left of his training. Therefore making him tougher and stronger than anyone before him. He was told that the other messengers thought the king was mad for increasing his training. Jared had almost died four times in the process. No-one could understand how he survived, but he did. The only thing that the king admitted to him was that it was in his blood to do so.

The king had kept Jared by his side at all times and on several occasions bid him stay in his own chambers as a child. In all his life Jared had only be sent on six missions, then the king started using magic like all the others. So why was Jared still here? Why was he not sent off like the others when the decree became final? Whatever the reason Jared was thankful. Throughout his life he became more than just a Royal Messenger. He acted as ambassador, spy, assassin and friend to the king. Now he again partook the roe of royal Messenger.

At the king's bidding to make hast, he did not delay for the lady in question was on her dying bed. His journey was not absolute and only a round-about location was known. He was to ask about an older lady, long gray hair who favored the color sky-blue and known only as G. She would have a young man with her who wore his hair long and only in a single braid. His travel to Woodberry would be at least a weeks travel, with any hinderance. Then he must find the lady and bring her back. He took with him only his weapons, a pouch of money, and his always trusty travel kit; consisting of lock picks, parchment and an ink well. But truly with the King's ring, he needed nothing else at all. He could go anywhere and ask for anything, show the ring and would not be denied.

As now when he entered the Coltain's tavern. He offered money for his food and bed but the barkeep refused to take it, "I will not put a bad name upon my tavern. Who would say that I charged the king's Royal Messenger." he said aloud to be heard by the early morning customers. Jared's outfit gave him away and then the king's ring clarified it.

He had rode all night and stopped only one to relieve his bladder. He desired to continue on but knew he needed the rest, being unprepared for the journey. He decided to get a bite to eat and only a few hours sleep, then he would head out again. His sleep would be a deep one, instituted by the Royal Messengers, one that would allow them to travel hard and fast at ease for days at a time without rest. But he also needed to thinking on somethings as well. Something was bothering him during his travel. He ate his sausage and potato and drank several mugs of water. Royal Messengers did not indulge in other drinks.

It was just two hours past dawn when he was lead to his room.

At dawn Lady Chelsey had crept to the far-east side of the rose garden and hood softly like an owl. When an answer was returned she stuck her hand through the stark bush there. There was a grinding sound, then a hand touched hers lightly and took the parchment from her hand. She rushed away and headed back inside to join in at the morning meal, for tit wold be announced soon. She was nervous and unsure if what the queen had told her was true. But being true to her word, there was an answer and a waiting hand to take her message.

"Lady Chelsey." a voice called from behind her.

She started but recovered herself quickly and turned to see Princess Elizabeth. They both gave a quick curtsy then Princess Elizabeth caught up with her. "Beautiful morning isn't it?"

"Well, yes it is." Lady Chelsey did not spend any time longer than she had to outside, paying no attention to how the new day began. But what else was she to say. She was far from her sleeping quarters and the dining hall. Lady Chelsey knew that the Princess had seen she was in a rush and was caught up to something. How was she to evade this meddling child? Her answer bumped into her as they turned the corner. "Oh my." she said startled again, but relieved to see it was her husband.

A hint of suspicion touched the princess' voice, "Lord Gregory?"

"Ah, there you are. I was afraid that you would not find the rose garden." Lord Gregory said. Both ladies looked at each other. "Well you did say that you wanted to see the rose garden, did you not?" he asked.

"Yes, yes I did. And they are just as beautiful as the queen said they would be." she caught on that her husband was saving her any embarrassing and uneasy talk with the princess.

"Well, that I am glad to hear." he faced the princess, "Good morning to be walking about, isn't my Princess?"

"Well, I would say that we all agree to that." she seen her chance alone with Lady Chelsey ruined and knew that she had no chance with Lord Gregory. "Do you know if the morning meal has started?" she asked.

"Shortly, that is why I came to find this early bird." he said looking from the Princess to his wife.

"Well then I shall accompany you there, if you don't mind."

"Oh of course not. You delight us, and I shall enjoy the company of my future daughter-in -law, and Queen." Lord Gregory said with a big smile.

The princess hugged him and said, "We shall see."

The three of them made their way to the dining hall undisturbed, speaking of the tourney the king and queen planned. Neither Lord Gregory nor Lady Chelsey bothered to ask where the Princess was coming from at such time in the morning.

At the dinning King Charles was the last to arrive and with an unexpected guess. Lord Robert walked in slowly with the aid of his cane. The elderly yet powerful man barely smirked when entering the presence of such a merry company. Being the eldest among the noble and very influential, and having spies aplenty; it was no surprise that he would show, only when was the question.

All stood upon the king's arrival and he waved his hand to seat them as he helped Lord Robert to an empty chair. "Isn't it just wonderful." he said when he finally eased down into his chair. "I came here to witness yet another royal engagement, and why look there. Is that my favorite great niece, Carmen?"

"It is I, your great niece Carmen; but favorite, come now Lord Robert." she said chuckling.

"Well, since my flattery of words will not accommodate for my in attendance in your life of late, then I openly apologize."

"Now that is the Uncle Lord Robert I remember."

That brought a soft laughter from them all. All ate and spoke of the up and coming events and tried to pretend that they did not notice the stares that both Lord Robert and King Charles laid upon certain guest.

There was suspicion and blame on the face of both men. But to what, no-one could guess or say why. Questioning stares and raised eyebrows between Princess Elizabeth and Caleb did not go unnoticed either, but again no-one mentioned it.

During the meal it was suggested by the princess that certain trivia be had at interval throughout the tourney. The king and queen both thought it a good idea. At the end of the meal as the table was being cleaned away and the party was excusing themselves for one reason or the other, the king said he would go unaccompanied foe a short walk to gather his thoughts. He would catch up to them before the competition began. Lord Robert left in the company of Lord Gregory and Lady instead of his great niece Lady Carmen. As expected he paid no more attention to her than he had in the past. His brother's second son's daughter was not of like mind with him and most knew it. Lady Carmen did share the views of her father's family. She was surprised when Lord Robert agreed on her marriage to Lord John. Lord John's family was just as powerful as Lord Robert's and Lord Wilford's, even though they were on opposite sides of politics. Because of a young Carmen's interest in politics and her out spokenness, she was more of a threat to Lord Robert's plans than an accomplice to his cause. But Carmen was a good spirited person and well liked, so her presence could not be ignored. Lord John's family was not only on the other side of politics but also on the opposite side of the king's land. Lord Robert thought it to be better if she was sent far away and not to cause a division among the household. So both Lord Robert and Carmen got what they wanted. She got the husband she wanted and he got rid of her.

The day was starting out very interesting.

6

A contingent of guards rode into Glassboro at noon and came upon the Coltian tavern. They immediately surrounded the place. Sentries were set about to watch windows and the back exit. Archers were put in place and customers outside were sent away. Two people quickly scaled the side of the building and were on the roof in no time. When all were in place, twelve men entered the Coltain. Two immediately guarded the door and no-one was allowed to leave. The band forced the people to silence but told the bard to keep playing. Rubyanne, the bar tender and her parents (the owners of the Coltian Tavern) were roughly set upon. They pleaded their innocence of anything and asked for mercy, but were silenced. A man wrapped in a hooded cloak, not to reveal himself, had stepped forward.

"The horse is outside. What room is he in, and is he alone?" the cloaked man asked in a calm plain voice.

There was confusion on the three captive faces, then Milly gasped with shock. She now realize who they spoke of, and they meant to do the Royal Messenger harm. Her family was at stake and she had no doubt that the Royal Messenger could fend for himself or slip out of a window and be on his way. Still she felt terrible to have to give him up. She hung her head and in a low voice she said, "He is in the second room on the left side." her husband tried to look at her but she adverted her eyes from him.

"Is he alone?"

"Yes. No-one went up with him."

"Put them in that corner over there" The hooded man pointed to the far side of the fireplace. Two men roughly pushed them about. "I want the three of you with your bows ready and do not hesitate to shoot on sight. The rest of you have your swords ready." His men rushed about to get good positions and the hooded man helped himself to the bar. "We will wait." he said.

Swords were drawn, bows were taunt with arrows set and more laid by at the ready. Their wait was shortly over half an hour.

Jared laid fully dressed in a comatose state, he didn't even appear to be breathing at all. There was no rise or fall of his chest. He laid on his back with his leg out straight. His left arm laid across his waist, his hand gripped the hilt of one of his black daggers. His right hand laid straight at his side where it held his short sword. He looked like a corpse laying at rest with his battle weapons ready to enter the next world. The sun had shifted to the right indicating its descent. It was no longer at its zenith and as if on signal and as if quickened from death, Jared's shirt pooped up as his heart reset its normal beat. His eyes shot opened and the grip on his short sword tightened; but he did not get up. Jared laid there listening. He took his hand from his dagger and sat up, lightly placing his feet on the floor. He looked at the short sword in his hand than laid it on the bed. He leaned forward placing his head in his hands and rubbing them over his head he tugged on his long braid at the back of his neck.

The look that the lady had given him was not good and if he remember her husband well enough he was a man that could tell his enemy that he hated him, his son that he loved him, and his wife good morning, while lying to the king without ever changing his facial expression. His face gave nothing away. But it did not mean all was well. Even though he did not see them he knew he heard several people come and go just as quickly before he made his own exit. But the lady... there was something of recognition on her face as she looked at him, or something on him. He would have to figure it out at another time.

Jared took a deep breath than stood his brow frowned as he quickly picked up his short sword and hurried lightly to the door. There was music but no other sound. This was a well-known tavern and it should be this quiet there wasn't even any noise outside of the place. He slid his short sword and its scabbard and drew his daggers, one in each hand. He stilled his nerves than opened the door and stepped out of the room. No-one was in the hallway or at the edge of the stairs but still Jared was uneased. He walked to the edge of the stairs and was turning to take the first step, a bow string thwanged than two more in rapid succession. He deflected the first two with his dagger and stepped back to avoid the third. Now there was an uproar of noise as men rushed his way. Several more arrows were sent his way and he thought to wait them out, but he heard a thump from down the hall. Someone had entered his room and would be coming his way soon. He had left the door to the room opened were he left just in case he needed to run back to it. But that was no longer a suggestion and may work against him. He quickly turned the corner and jumped the stairs, deflecting arrows on his way to the floor. He landed lightly on his feet in a crouch and threw both daggers.

Two of the archers fell and he drew his short sword and a star from his waist. Immediately flicking it at the third archer. The archer ducked behind a table guarding himself from the objects. The others wasted no time in attacking Jared and he met them head on.

Raising his sword he parried an attack from one man, lifted his left arm to block another man's attack. That man was surprised to hear metal meet metal when his sword made contact with Jared's left arm. Jared rushed him bringing his left hand horizontal with the man's shoulder and flexed his wrist. A short blade shot out from his wrist and Jared stabbed the man in the throat. Another quick flex and the blade retracted. He pushed the man into another attacker and focus in on the first one. Their swords were locked and only Jared's eyes were in his direction. He seen the other men coming and decided not to struggle with this one. There may still be more upstairs. He kicked the man in the knee breaking it back, the man howled in pain and Jared stuck his sword in him lifting up as the man fell. Ducking from a swing to his head, he brought up his sword to block another attack in one fluid motion as he extracted it from the gut of the fallen man. As the men came and pressed him with attacks, Jared pressed back. His blocks, twist and turns made him look like a wild dancer.

Jared quickly stomped the heel of his boot on the floor, a blade sprang out and he kicked out making contact with one man to his underarm as he raised his sword to swing. Twisting from that kick and never letting his foot hit the ground, he kicked another man in the side. Jared had enough room to tuck and roll forward, allowing himself more room away from the stairs. As he bent to do so his left hand quickly grabbed and let fly two stars. Taking one man in the eye and grazing another on the ear. Only four men were truly out of the fight and as Jared seen when he jumped the stairs, the two men at the door; one guarding the tavern owners and the one behind the bar had not joined the fight as yet. He had to be rid of these four men before any others came in or down the stairs.

Jared was well trained and in control of himself and his weapons. These four men would only serve as mere sport, a warmer. Still he did not want to be caught off guard. He allowed himself to feel the ecstasy of the fight and with just a brush of it excited pleasure. He dropped his short sword and exploded into the men with just hands and feet. A touch to one man's shoulder paralyzed him. A flex of his wrist and a blade sprang out cutting the jugular of another. A combination of kicks and upper cuts broke a leg, popped an arm and snapped a neck. The next man's forward motion helped Jared pull him further down meeting a raising knee. Jared grabbed him, twisted him lifting him in the air to let him forcefully drop onto an awaiting knee that broke his back. He quickly pushed the man away, retrieved his short sword and speared it at the man coming down the stairs, striking him in the throat. No-one rushed him as he surveyed the room and the four remaining men. Jared straightened his cape and went to retrieve his daggers. He snatched the first one out of the up turned table and felt a tingling in his temple. Someone was trying to use magic on him. He was immune to its use upon his person, something they obviously didn't know. He bent to pull his other dagger from the eye of a dead man, upon standing a table flew across the room knocking him down. In his fall he threw a star at the man guarding the tavern owner striking him deep in the throat. The man's hands shot to his neck as he struggled to breathe but choked on his own blood.

Jared waited for another attack but none came. He heard running feet up the stairs and pushed the table from him to see three remaining men were gone. He collected himself and went to get the rest of his weapons. Jared picked up a bow and some arrows the archers had. He was good with the bow, but didn't like it. It took away from the close up contact. "I apologize for the..." he started but Milly ran to him crying and fell at his feet begging is forgiveness.

"Oh, it was me! I told them you were up stairs. I, I feared for my family. You must forgive me. You must! Oh!" she cried.

"You are not at fault. They knew I was here and would have either come up or waited here like they had." he dropped several coins from his pouch into her hands and went to the door. Jared readied the bow and stepped out. He stayed close to the building as he scanned his surroundings. He could just barely see the hidden sentries in and behind trees, peeking and stealing glances his way. They were well enough off in the forest that the normal man would not have seen them. He was about to check on his horse but the noticed a small crowd of huddled people off to the side of him. There was a child among them and he kept looking up at the roof. Whether they knew it or not, whoever was up there just lost any chance of surprise. He eased back inside and seen Milly and Rubyanne straightening out the tavern. He quickly, yet lightly ran pass them and headed up the stairs. He wasted no time climbing out the window and onto the roof. He immediately set the bow and fly two arrows repeatedly into the back of the men who waited to ambush him. Where they fell over, he went to that side and alighted from the roof onto the stable roof then the ground. A volley of arrows assailed him. He swatted them away with his bow and wrist guard before making it into the stable. There stood two men awaiting him with sword in hand. They rushed him with yells and he quickly silenced them as they fell lifelessly to the ground. He faced his horse, it flared its nostrils and whined. It too was ready for action.

Jared opened the stable door and instead of climbing on his horse, he ran beside it full out the stable and into the forest. Jared let fly arrow after arrow as he ran alongside his horse. The horses garment protected its chest and flanks from the arrows sent its way. Foe fell out of trees, others stuck to them with an arrow in their arm or at the throat or shoulder. When the arrows ran out he drew his sword. Only five men met him head on. His horse ran down one, stopped suddenly and back kicked another. Jared quickly twisted, turned, slashed and chopped down the other three men. No others attacked.

Jared standing just over six feet, walked beside his horse for a while ready and alert. He was about two hundred and ten pounds, slim at the waist and all muscle in fluent motion. When he was younger and the other royal Messengers were about, they called him Autan; in the old language it meant rushing water. He allowed himself a slight smile. His square jaw and light beard resembled all the Royal Messengers and even though he was the last of his people he never forgot them. And he was kind of happy to have a mission again.

As he climbed on his horse and galloped off he stayed alert. He knew whose men were sent after him and he knew they would not let up that easy. They would meet up again. The gripped bleeding heart emblem burned deep in his mind. It was ashamed that he was forbidden two things as a Royal Messenger. One, if his attackers were not caught in action; he could not report them. Even though in action he could kill them. Two, a Royal Messenger could never seek revenge. They were already thought unpredictable, incontrolable, inhuman, deadly and unstoppable. He heard it all. But a Royal Messenger's life was not his own and he was only a pawn in the scheme of royal politics. A living game of chest. As he rode on he thought, if he was his own man with a family, would he seek out revenge then or would he still play the political game.

7

Jared rode into Washington the next day. He rode hard the last day and a half expecting another attack but no-one followed or jumped out. He didn't need the rest but his horse was exhausted and whining heavy. He thought to exchange his horse so that he could continue on, but his horse was very trusting and good in battle. Just a few hours rest then he would feed it the elixir. An herb magically enhanced with just a drop. He kept this elixir in a special made ring. With this feed the horse would be refreshed and ready for hard riding, two days of it. He knew the area and didn't need to stop and ask for directions or any other questions. He got off his horse and walked for an hour or so. They came upon Blackwood Tavern and upon seeing him, people readily moved out of his way. Royal Messengers did not have good reputations, even though they don't attack people or fight unless someone tries to harm them. He was used to thus reaction so he paid them no mind. He asked for his horse t be tended to and a stable boy came to take his horse. The boy's eyes lit up when he seen the rare breed of the Appaloosian from Creaton. A big well-muscled horse known for their battle furry, speed, and endurance. Jared seen the surprise in the boy's face and patted his horse. "Take care of my baby, she's an old one now."

"Yes, ye...yes sir." the boy stuttered leading the horse away.

Jared was restless so he walked the town revisiting places he had already been. He reach the only river the next town had. He scooped up its water splashing his face then he drank deep. It was cold and refreshing. He shrugged his shoulder then he stripped off his cloths and stepped into the cold water. His flesh goosed up and his breath caught just a bit but it felt good as he plunged into the cold water. He quickly bathed himself but kept watchful eye of his surroundings. People seen him coming this way and he knew that it wasn't the towns people he would have to worry about. But if they told of his location guards would-be attackers came, he didn't want to be caught with his clothes off.

The first thing he put on was his wrist guard. The blade attached to it and its spring trap were well oiled and set right. Its blade was sharp and ready. He wore regular under garments but put on tightly meshed knee guards very flexible but hard. He wore a mail shirt made by the dwarfish people of the snow caps. There work was renown and very expensive to foreigners. His leather pants and over shirt was tough material. His boots had its spring blade, his cape too had special blades sewn into the corner seams. Next where his daggers and stars, short sword then long blade. He had never took off his ring with the potions in them. Jared thought on all these things and his years of special training as he dressed and headed back. How did so many of the Royal Messenger die when they were released from duty? There was several that was not only tough fighters but smart and head strong. They had the knowledge, and since they were no longer duty bound by rules they could have trained an army and taken over any land, just about. It may have taken quite some years but still it could have been done. And who was there to stop them.

Jared received quick glances, long stares and whispered conversation all the way back and into the tavern. He walked to a back table and the three sitting there got up and left. He adjusted his cape and sat down. From there he could see every part of the tavern, the entry, windows, steps, behind the counter and when someone came out of the back from the kitchen or storage.

Jared set and waited and thought on a lot of things he was uncertain of. He fought a long time allowing his mind to wonder with different scenarios. The hushed whispers, the rushed servants, the stares, the attack on him, what did they have in common. It could not have been a coincidence. There were noble people's guards after him, from a family that did not even attend the party. Well none that he seen or heard of their arrival. They could not have just been waiting for him to leave the castle all this time. How did they even know he had a mission and where he was headed? It did not add up in his mind. He shook his head and thought about his horse to clear his mind. He would feed her then walk for a while before riding her again.

He went to the bar and requested of any dried sausage meat for travel, two days-worth. The barkeep rushed in the back to get what he requested. He thought, sometimes it would be nice to be asked about his welfare or how his day went, while other people sat beside him and tried to ignore him. Thus, the lonely life of a Royal Messenger traveling. He missed the comfort and company of the castle. The barkeep came back with a wrapped bundle of sausage meat. Saying nothing she slid it in front of him.

Jared thanked her and left a coin on the table as he walked away. He went to the stable and his horse neighed tossing her head up in the air, she was happy to see him and well rested. The stable boy had relieved her of her saddle and Jared could smell lather sent of soap. The boy had bathe d her as well. He seen that the boy had sat down and nodded off in the corner and thought to let him sleep. From the horses saddle he produced a small pouch that he took the herbs from and crushed them in his hand. Then he twisted the top of his ring and let a drop of the liquid fall into it. Taking several handfuls of hay, (he always remembered to keep some with him) he mixed them up and fed it to his horse who expectantly chomped it up. He rubbed her back and patted her side. She neighed and this time the sleeping boy jumped up and was startled to see Jared standing there with the horse. The bot stood up stammering. "I, I, I'm sorry, sir."

Jared turned to him, "For what lad?"

"I, I...well she is a lot of horse to wash and, and I nodded off. I fell asleep, sir, I'm sor..."

"It's alright, no foul done." Jared said going to get the saddle.

"I'll do it." the lad spoke up. Then added, "Sir."

Jared had seen that the boy was happy and eager to care for the horse. He knew that he would brag for some time to come about this so Jared let him. "Well, carry on then."

The boy smiled and set the saddle on the big horse. He struggled a bit but managed on his own and was proud of himself. "Can I walk her out, sir?"

"Lead on." Jared said and followed him out of the sable. The boy had a hard time trying not to smile. Jared seen that he wanted to look important and serious as he lead a Appaloosian horse out. Whether it was for just the horse or to be seen leading the Royal Messenger's horse he could not tell. Jared allowed himself a brief smile to cross his own face before he too stepped out of the barn behind him. The boy looked up at him and he nodded his head and pointed for the boy to continue on. The boy gave a slight nod, stood tall and walked on. They walked quietly away from the tavern for a few minutes then the boy stopped.

He said softly dropping his head, "My parents would not wish me to go any further, sir." he lifted his head, "but I will if you..."

"No, no." Jared stopped him. "This is fine. Obey your parents and head on back." He produced two coins from his pouch, "Give one to your parents and keep one for yourself." he took hold of his horse thanking the boy before he proudly walked off. Both knew that he was being watched, by his peers mostly.

Jared walked on well away from the tavern and out of town. He followed the river until it turn off. Stopping to drink again and let his horse do the same as well. For a couple more hours he walked on letting his horse have plenty of rest. He knew that he would be riding hard for some time and the horse would be doing all of the work, running and carrying him. The evening was now coming in fast and Jared decided to ride on and catch as much light as he could. He climbed on his horse and pressed his knees into her and she picked up a trot and another press and then a gallop. Half an hour later he pressed again into her sides and she sprinted head long until the sun fell. At an even pace he brought her back to a trot. Their travel was undisturbed which brought Jared's mind back to the attack at the last tavern. They had liked to press him, or was that some type of test. But why, for what? Why attack him like that then leave him be? There wasn't even any trace of a scout about, no-one trailing him or anything. He let the thought pat, no reason to dwell on it. His stomach growled then he remembered the sausage bundle and raced to retrieve it. With no hesitation he tore into them.

He continued on and the night was pleasant, normal with its night activity. Nothing was amiss, but his horse began to neigh and toss her head about. He looked for any signs of trouble but hi vision began to blur and his stomach turned. The reigns in his hands began to loosen from his grip and he leaned forward on his horse. No wander there were no scouts about. They had already guest he would be coming this way, knew that he would want food for travel. The dried sausage meat was already prepared for him. All they needed to do was wait for the necessity to set in. he had not thought that they would poison his food. Foolish – was his last thought before he passed out.

8

"This is madness!" King Gaston says as he paces back and forth behind the empty chair. "How long must we wait?"

"We are guess here Gaston and something has befallen Charles, so we must wait until it has been lifted. I am sure it's just a day bug; something short lasting. But whatever it is, it will pass and we will pick up where we left off. So calm yourself." Queen Beatrice told him.

He threw up his hands in the air and gave up any argument he thought to conjure. She was right, they were guest in another kingdom and if they must wait, it shant be long. Well he had hoped so anyway as he walked around and plopped in the chair he was just pacing behind a few minutes ago.

Almost everyone was here and it looked as if things would began his morn, the last day of the tourney. Of course they would have to make up or start from where they stopped yesterday evening. No-one has seen King Charles since their mid reprieve during the tourney. It was obvious that something has been amiss with him and he was greatly distracted, but he confided in no-one. Since that Jared fellow made his damned appearance that night in the hall, the king has not been himself since.

King Charles tried to put on a good face for his guest but it had become too much for him. He seemed to be watching with suspicious eyes and everything he said seemed to be guarded. He did not trust himself to say much to anyone as if someone would misuse his words or learn too much. But it wasn't just him, the Princess Elizabeth had seemed drawn back from the event as well. Oh she played her part, but it was not genuine. She knew something that she was not revealing and seemed to be guarding herself from everyone as well itself to her.

The rest of the party seem to moving about as if all were fine but King Gaston was not convinced. He knew that something was about and was glad it had nothing to with him whatever it was, it was civil issue among themselves and he was glad to leave it that way. He sat in his chair and looked about suitors for the princess. There were huddled among themselves and appeared to be behaving, even though they were in competition for the same goal. The had bested each other in various competition, all but that Caleb he was by himself, he had not been a part of their group conversation at all and truthfully King Gaston thought the other four suitors conspired against him; but he always held his ground.

As the king now sat and watched them, Conrad- his son seemed on edge about something. For a while now the scowl on his face was as if he just learned that he had been duped. Something was out of his control and he didn't like what it was, what he had just learned. He wanted to argue with the other three but stopped himself. He was a strong and confident man and was ready to rebut anything not agreeable, unfair or just out of his understanding. It had seemed as what was a victory just turned out to be a deal through default, trickery and under handedness. He realized he had been used. King Gaston knew that look well and his son turned accusing eyes from his companions to him. What has he done to deserve this gazed? King Gaston stood as his son Prince Conrad approached him.

"What is the meaning of your look boy?" He challenged

"If I thought it would not disgrace my people I would leave here now. But I will play my part in your scheme just this last time."

King Gaston grabbed his arm before he turned to leave, "Do you accused me of something and not speak your mind boy? I demand to know."

"As if you do not know." his voice was tight. "A win is win, but I will not play a part in treachery."

King Gaston's grip tightened on Prince Conrad's arm as he brought him closer to him, "Speak your mind boy or I will strike you here and now,"

"You taught me to win a fight you do what you must while you are in it. There is no cheating during the fight to win." Prince Conrad now stood as if he was the one giving the lecture to his child on fairness. "It is unjust to plan ahead to dupe your foe before the battle begins. I will go against that now."

"And who implies that you do?" King Gaston demanded.

"And now you hide in my face father?" Prince Conrad demanded back.

King Gaston hand raised as if to strike his son but he held back. He recalled his surroundings and would not disgrace his son and heir here in a foreign land. Prince Conrad had seen it but will not flinch from him.

"Would you force me to conspire, to feign victory on a defeated foe, cheated so?

"A cheated foe?" The King was now confused and it showed clearly on his face. The Prince chanced a glance about the dias his mother seated apart from other Queens and ladies. She tried not to look, to stair their way. She seemed not a part of the others, as though left out.

How had his father fit in with the others? How did he respond to his challenge? And now he seems ignorant. It had now become clear to Prince Conrad that his parents were not in on the 'our parents have decided it best' comment the other suitors made. They, the Creatons were not a part of it. Breaking his train of thought his father asked him again.

"A cheated foe? Speak Conrad."

"You don't know. But the said our..." Prince Conrad looked pass his father again and at the group of royal and noble parents. His was truly not a part of this nor were Caleb's. "We need to speak privately just you and I." he told his father and gestured that they moved on from where they were standing. He led the way and King Gaston followed.

When the two of them departed, Caleb too left, saying nothing to no-one. He headed inside the castle looking for Princess Elizabeth. Princess Bethel had eased off behind him. As he made his way on he realized that he had an extra shadow. Princess Bethel was besotted with him of late and made no pretense at hiding it, and now she followed him. Caleb had stopped and turned to her, he thought to end this charade here and now before it got out of hand.

"Princess, may I help you with something?" he asked her as she continued her way toward him.

She was not surprised that he turn to find her there. No man of his skill and prowess could have not known that she was being trailed. "Where do you go off to?" she asked.

"A private matter."

"You seek the Princess?"

"I may."

"She does not want you. Why do you fight for her?" the princess had seemed a bit bashful at first, yet determined. But her last question was bold.

"I do as I must. As we all do."

"So, must you be part of unhappiness? It is clear that the two of you do not want this union. Yet you fight the hardest among those who want what you do not."

"It is better to choose what is right over our own happiness. A true ruler, king, will think of those that he rules before himself. For without the ruled there is no ruler. So my actions are for the greater cause, one that will succeed

45

myself, for what I will gain I must leave behind. Shall I do an injustice to those that will take my place? A kingdom is more than just a king, so I do as I must."

Princess Bethel stood there thinking on what he said. She would love to have him by her side. He was a man of ponderance and one that you could be sure in battle. He spoke justly even though it seemed confusing and at odds with a desired effect of simple pleasure. He was the one to remind you that there is always the side of business and duty. A conscious reminder at odds with itself warning those of temptation but being a tempter of its own. His face was serious but handsome all the same. "Must you not take foolish chances in life sometimes?" she asked him.

"We all do. But should it be on purpose?" he asked in return.

"I think just to seek the outcome, sometimes yes."

"But if the outcome, once done cannot be change; would you stand proudly to be blamed. Or to know the ill effect it has caused to all else?"

"So you believe that one man shall suffer for the greater cause of others?"

"I would say for others, not because of others."

"Then you are saying that all are not responsible for their own actions? Who is then to stand proudly at blame for something to get no credit for the deed? Where is the pride in accepting false accusations? Just man, where then is the justice?" she challenged.

Caleb thought she just twisted his own words, then threw them back at him. His own justice, his since of duty challenged by his own mind. "Justice is higher than the one delivering it. It exist in its own right and will outlast its distributors. The recipients ask not where it came from yet they marvel in it."

"Then they are sick. They are unbalanced and disturbed to know that they rejoice in sufferance. To laugh when one cries. To shed tears of joy and applaud the affliction and doom of the fallen. Ignorance is not excuse and pleasure is not reason to stay in such a state. If so, then it is purposely done. If you know that you cannot be blamed for your ignorance, then why become responsible? Live life and take foolish chances. Who knows, someone else might volunteer to take the blame. You know, out of since of duty." she leaned in and kissed him lightly on the lips then turned away leaving him standing there. He watched her a moment then shook his head and went his own way. She is the typical female, beautiful, yet confusing.

Caleb wondered around the castle, speaking when greeted but kept it brief and sticking to his course. He didn't want to outwardly say that he sought the princess so he wandered till he found her pacing the hall in front of a closed door. She looked worried, unsure, and did not hear his footsteps approach.

Princess Elizabeth paced in front of the door, fighting a fear that all in the castle had. She knew that she was possibly mad to even think about this, to come this close, to be here even this long. But still she had not approach the door to open it, and she knew that she would not. So why was she still here? This was nothing new for her father. He had frequently visited this place aplenty and had come out only when he was ready to regardless to anything. So why had she come? The reason clenched tightly in her hand and she glanced down at it as she paced. It was important that the king be told this information. So why was she hesitating? She turned and seen a shadow in front of her and looked up to see Caleb standing there.

"Oh, Caleb, what are you doing here?

"I came to see about you and what was taking you so long to return."

"Caleb, you will draw attention. You must go back."

"It is too late for that, Princess Bethel has already caught me."

"What?"

"I sent her away, or more or less she left. But anyway there is too much going on back there that no-one else will come this way."

"What happened?"

"Nothing much. It is the same with the huddled groups. I think that something has upset Prince Conrad and he could not bear it."

"What has he done? I knew he could not resist incivility. The Prince is too bar..."

"Now hold on Elizabeth. He has done nothing out right 'uncivil'. He went to the king, his father, and they had a heated conversation. Before I came to search you out they walked off to speak privately, nothing more."

Elizabeth looked around uncertain still. She took Caleb's hand and led him away from the door. "Caleb I do not like this. What if they manage to kill Jared? Or what will happen if the Princess comes back here?"

"That is not for us to decide. Your father will handle the situation. But as I see it, you have not given him your letter yet. Why?"

She looked down at it, still clutched in her hand. "I... I don't know what this will cause."

"That is not for you to worry about. Elizabeth, the king must know. You must warn him what he is up against."

"I know Caleb." her soft voice raised an octave. She was frustrated and uncertain. She did not want to be the reason of any unrest in the kingdom for surely this letter will cause unrest.

"Give it here." Caleb extended his hand for it.

"What?"

"The letter, give it to me."

She looked at him uncertain but lifted her hand and the letter to him. He reached for it but she would not let it go.

"Elizabeth."

"But Caleb, what if..."

"Don't worry about that." Elizabeth released the letter. He seen that it was not sealed but it had her signature on it. Caleb opened it and seen it was two full sheets of her writing. He did not read it, but closed it up and walked to the door.

"Caleb what are you..."

He raised his hand to silence her. With quick steps he approached the door and before she could stop him, he slid the letter hard under the door.

"Caleb you had no right!" she said hitting him on the shoulder.

He turned to her holding her in both hands. "Now you listen to me Princess, we are not children anymore. We are adults now and have duties. You more so than me at the moment. There is no time for us to hesitate about. The responsibilities of the kingdom may fall on our shoulders one day and I for one know that you do not wish to be a puppet ruler or in the middle of a civil revolt. It may seem foolish to interfere but you know that it is right."

"But you..."

"It is done now and the king will know."

She didn't know what to say. She had not guessed that he would do that. She would have done the same thing, but she needed just a little more time.

"You may want to leave and prepare yourself for the kings response. Whatever it may be, or do you wish to be here when that door opens?"

She looked at the door and knew that he was right. She turned and walked off, Caleb followed.

9

He was moving but did not know it. He had no feeling in any of his limbs. He could hear the dragging of something on the ground. He tried to concentrate just to open his eyes but it was impossible to even do that. He was only aware that he was barely alive and could faintly hear. Nothing else. But he knew that something was being dragged. He tried to remember what happened to him. How he could not see, or fell anything. He couldn't even smell and was barely able to think. Blackness covered him and now even his thoughts and awareness faded.

Jared's body lay twitching on a stack of hay. His eyelids continuously fluttering, his hands clenched and his stomach made noise. His body jerked up and vomit shot out his mouth his hands involuntarily wrapped around himself as he wretched. His body barely straightened before he bent over and wretched again. His eyes never opened as he laid limped again.

"Will this ever pass?" a young girl said as she wrung out another cloth and placed under Jared neck. She took another cloth and wiped the sweat and vomit from his face and mouth. She had thought to unclothed him and put him in a tub for he was burning with fever. But her father forbid it.

She did not know who he was or why he was dressed so, but her father did her to not touch anything about him. She was instructed to not let him choke on his own vomit and to keep putting cold rags behind his neck. This poor man suffered dearly and there was nothing more she could do for him.

Jared passed in and out of awareness time and time again, but this time his awareness was more acute. He could hear horses and sheep neighing. He could smell and the odor was foul, but he still could not move his limbs. He did not have a headache but his stomach was in terrible pain. He let his mind roam over his body assessing himself. He knew he was in a foul state and that the odor was him. He had soiled himself and could now feel the ill of it on him. Urine and feces was strong in his nostrils, and vomit. His memory shot back and he knew he was poisoned it was the sausages he ate, and he fell over on his horses neck. But where was he now?

He could hear the dripping of water as if being wrung from something. His eyes felt heavy and swollen but he managed to open them. As he did so he felt a cold cloth wiping his forehead. The movement paused as the wiper realized that his eyes were open. It was hard for him to focus but he could see a face surrounded by hair, or was it a hood.

"Oh my." The voice from the face said than they were both gone, face and voice. He tried to speak but his throat was to dry and painful. The voice came back and with it another.

"They are still open. He keeps his awareness father." a female voice said.

"Calm yourself and let me see him." a man spoke. Than the face he first saw came into view. It was a young girl with dark tresses who stood before him and alongside it was a bearded one- her father.

"Yes, I see his eyes are open. Go and get another rag. And some clean water too, some for him to drink. He should be thirsty." The father told the girl and her face quickly disappeared. "Royal Messenger, can you her me?" The man asked.

Jared tried to speak, wanted to desperately but could not yet move his lips and had not yet found his voice. The man had seen this and spoke again.

"If you can hear me just blink and I will know." Jared managed to. "That is good. Okay um, sorry that I had to leave you in such a state. But I fear to touch your person. My daughter has kept a cool rag under your neck and whipped your face. I ask your permission to let my daughter remove your weaponry and clothing so she can clean you. I um, well you can blink twice for no or once for yes. You are in a foul state, um Royal Messenger sir."

Jared understood the man's weariness, for no one touched a Royal Messenger ever and no one ever helped one either. He was taking a grave chance with himself and family. Normally Jared would not accept any help but he had never been in a situation such as this before. He was not too proud of a man to accept help from another when he knew he needed it. Jared knew his own plight and embarrassment. No one but another Royal Messenger has ever seen him fully unclothed. It was more than just having no clothes. For all Royal Messenger's bodies were a work of art not seen by the public. The girl and her father would later be sworn to secrecy all their life, or Jared, if they spoke about him would be in grave danger if they remember his markings. Even when he bathed in the river he made sure that no one was around to see him. But he must put all that aside now, he must take a chance. Jared blinked once.

"I will see to it that you have plenty of water." The man said and got up. His daughter returned, "I have been given permission for you to remove his clothing and weaponry. Bathed him first than ask about his belongings. He has not yet recovered his voice, so if you ask him anything make sure it is a yes or no question. He will blink twice for no and once for yes. Give him drink and see how that helps him out. I will return with a tub and water."

The young nodded as her father instructed her. When he left she came and sat by Jared. She wiped his brow and under his neck. She poured water in a small tin cup and was about to rise it to him but realized that it would not work. The man's lips were too dry and cracked looking to move and he appeared to be unable to move them anyway. She put the cup down and instead picked up another rag. Pouring water on it she brought it to Jared's mouth, pressing it against his lips. She didn't know if could even swallow but he managed to as the water wet his lips and filled his mouth.

He never drank anything other than water and he never took its taste for granted, or so he thought. The cold liquid was a life saver. Cold and delicious, it was a reviver for him. The girl asked if he wanted more and he blinked once for yes. Over and over she drenched the cloth and brought it to his mouth only to stop because there was no more. His eyes were clearer and his lips moistened. The water filled him up and he could feel and he could feel his body drawing it from his stomach to much need parts.

The girl continued to wipe his face and neck. She was nervous and did know how to start removing his clothing. Her trembling hands started by unclasping his cape from his neck and she let it fall limp. Slowly she removed his daggers and stars. His short sword she unstrapped then untied his money bag. Neatly she lay everything out next to each other on the ground. His boots and socks slid off his feet. Then slowly peeled off his shirt. By the time she had gotten to his underpants her father had brought in two tubs of water and blankets. They were dragged in on a litter by one of the mules. Once they were in place her father left again. Jared was no small man but she managed to get him into the tub by herself. She was not yet a grown woman, but she was strong from farm work. She maneuvered him as if he were one of the sheep or farm animals. She picked up the rough soap and after lathering the wet cloth she began to bath him.

The water she gave him to drink did wanders for his lips, throat and innards. And now the water he bath in was cleaning his outside. He was grateful for the help he was getting but he still didn't like to feel helpless to himself. This was one of those times he wished he could seek revenge. He would make them all pay for doing this to him. None of his thought were pleasant as he lay there being bath by this strange but helpful young lady. Once she had thoroughly bathed him, she lifted him from the tub and placed him in the other one. Letting him soak and relax she left the shed and was gone for some time.

Jared lay there trying out the use of his fingers and toes. The only part of his body he was able to move were his eyelids. Slowly he could feel more and more parts of his body coming to life, but he still had no control of it as yet. The young lady returned with her father, both carried big pails of waters. She came and gave him more water, then she sat down and began to clean his clothing. By the time she finished washing and hanging up his clothing, Jared was able to move his wrist and ankles. He clenched the muscles in his jaws repeatedly and managed to open his mouth slightly. But he still had no voice, he couldn't even moan. The effects of the poison were wearing off and that relieved him greatly. His body was fighting it as it was trained to do. But with the help of this young lady giving him drink and rubbing his muscles while she bathed him aided in the healing process.

He had wondered how long he was unconscious once he passed out on his horse. Where was his horse and how did he get here anyway. Wherever here was. Now he wondered how much time had passed. Would the princess he sought still be alive? Where were the people that did this to him? Were they on to her as well? It would do no good worrying about it, not in the condition he was in now. He could do nothing for her or himself. He shut his eyes and fell into himself. His mind and will was still strong, so he focused them on parts of his body. Falling into his meditation slumber he let his body heal. Only the smell of cooked meat brought him out of it. Until then he hadn't realized how hungry he was. His mouth watered and his stomach growled loudly, shocking himself, the young lady and her father who had brought the tray in and was standing watch over him. A slight smile creased his face.

"I take it that you are hungry. I had thought that some good cooked meat would help you as well. You are recovering better with the help of water alone. But with something solid I believe you would be up in no time."

Jared had not yet tried his voice nor had he made any movement. He just lay there looking at the man.

"I do not wish to hurry your recovery," the man said in a low voice lowering his head. "But I am no fighter" he looked to his daughter then back to Jared. "If the people who did this to you start to search out your body, I; I would be little help to defend you. My daughter is the only family I have. I, I'm sorry Royal Messenger but I do not wish to see her harmed because we was foolish enough to interfere." He paused for a moment then turned to his daughter.

He brushed the hair from her face then lay a hand on her shoulder. "She will continue to see you." He then walked out of the shed.

The young lady moved about the shed and Jared watched her with his eyes.

"My father has prepared a tub of hot water" she said coming back to him.

"I will put you in it. Maybe it will help out with your muscles. While you soak I will cut up your food smaller so that it will go down easier. Your clothes have been taken to dry by the hearth. Mr. um, Royal Messenger sir, my father does fear greatly for us and truly does wish you a speedy recovery." she moved him into the other tub and the heated water sent sensations and ease to his muscles immediately. She gave him more drink then stood over him looking down on him. "I think you should know, my father has spent a great deal of time covering the tracks your house made in dragging you here. There have been men looking for you already. But my father knows of a strong herb that is strong enough to hide the scent of you and your horse. The hounds won't track you here. But your horse does not like it much" she said smiling. "But she is smart and tolerates the smell. My father washed and fed her, he tends to her while I tend to you. It is only a matter of time before the one looking for you figure it out. We have intended in matters that does not concern us and my father says you well know it. We should have let you be." She started to say more, but knew she would get no response. She turned from him and worried herself with his food.

The warm water soothed him and he flexed his muscles underneath it. He tightened and loosened his fingers and now managed to turn his head. The young lady sat on a bale of hay with her back to him. But he could tell what she was doing. She tore the meat into smaller pieces and her body turned slightly as she placed them in a bowl of steaming water. Soup he thought and again his mouth watered and his stomach growled drawing the attention of the young lady. She turned to him and seen him facing her.

The warm water and thought of water is doing you well. I can see that once you get something solid in you, you will recover more quickly." she paused in the thought then said. "I have never seen such a thing, but my father said this is no great fate for you, A Royal Messenger. That this is only a part of who you are, or what you can do. He said that if we had left you alone, you would have healed eventually. We are just speeding the process. "She turned back to what she was doing but continued to speak. "My father says that there are many people who believe that the Royal messenger cannot die. Or that they have evil spirits in them that make them hard to kill." She paused for a moment and Jared knew what she had to say. "Is it true? Is that the reason you have all those markings on you?" she knew that Jared was conscious and that he could hear her well, but she spoke on not worrying about a response, other than him just looking at her. As she stirred the meat into the bowl Jared could smell vegetables too. Onion and something else. Potatoes? Yes potatoes. The young lady came to kneel beside the tub and Jared's stomach rolled and growled as if it would attack her. "Can you move your mouth yet?" She asked.

Jared nodded his head yes and even more, when she put the bowl down to set him up straight he was able to push up with his arms. It taxed him greatly but he did it. Once he was sitting up straight she begin to spoon feed him the soup. She had chopped up the onion, potatoes and meat so small that he barely had to chew. The hot meal was soothing his throat and warming him up on the way down, relieving the pain in his stomach. She fed him the whole bowl and he drank the broth. When done she told him she was removing him from the tub. They had prepared a bed of straw for him and lay blankets about to cover him while his clothes dried. As soon as his head touched the hay he was asleep.

Again Jared awoke to the smell of hot food. This time when his eyes opened he sat up without even thinking about it but then felt the strain of it. He surveyed himself and could feel that everything was painfully working. He even managed a groggy sound. This drew the attention of both the young lady and her father. When the young lady turned Jared could see that her father held his clothing folded in his arms, and she a bowl of food.

"Royal Messenger sir, you have come along greatly. I am glad to see you sitting up on your own. Your recovery has taken just over half a day, by evening you should be on your way."

A half of day? It felt like forever. But Jared knew it was due to their care that he recovered so fast, and that he would somehow have to find a way to repay them.

The man told him not to waste his voice or strain to much of his strength. "Your clothing and weaponry are right here beside you and I will bring you your horse", leaving her just outside here. "We will leave you now and when you are ready you may depart." they turned to leave but the young lady stopped.

"You do not have to worry about us. We will not say a thing about what we saw or what happened to you. As far as my father concerned once you leave, you were never here."

Jared ate the food and drank from a jug left to him. He sat further and slowly bent his legs and arms circulating his blood flow. When he felt confident he reached for his clothing. As much as he could dress himself while sitting down he did. But he had to rest before he placed his weaponry about him. His movements were slow and stiff and he was still not fully recovered but he could move enough to leave this place. He managed to stand for a few minutes but had to sit back down. His body really was not ready yet.

The girl returned to the shed with a bundle in her hand. "My father says that you should have this, it is meat and bread. You should be well enough not to eat from anyone for two or three days, depending on your appetite. You should be able to find water on your own."

Jared was about to say something, to thank her but she stopped him.

"There is no need for thanks or any words. My father just ask that you remember that we are loyal to the king." she handed him the bundle and walked off.

Jared walked out of the shed at night fall. He left three gold coins on the bowl and set it on the bale of hay. He slowly climbed upon his horse and turned her in the direction he wished to go. He leaned upon her as she slowly carried him away. Revenge he could not seek, but the favor of the king upon someone he could request. He would remember the aid they gave him.

10

He let the cub leap from his arms as his face twisted into a frown. Who in their right mind would go against his command? There was no sounds of war or an invasion, so who would disturb him. This was his time to reminisce, to mentally degrade himself of his own cowardice, to go through all of the what if possibilities and what should be. To remind himself to never ever let something even remotely similar happen again.

Everyone knew that he came here and that he was not to be bothered. He alone had the only key to this room and he alone ever entered. No-one on pains of death could enter here and disturb this room. A habit he picked up from his father. The contents of the room was the same ever since he could remember. He alone like his father before him only dusted the place and brushed away the cobwebs, opened the window every now and then to air the lace out. They disturbed nothing else themselves. Now someone had approached the door and done something to draw the attention of the cubs, which alerted him.

King Charles walked to the door following the cub. It had swatted at something a few times before the king realized what it was. It was a letter. A letter someone had slid under the door. The letter slid past his feet as the cub gave it swat and bounced after it again. He turned it over and seen the delicate hand writing of his daughter. Princess Elizabeth, she had neatly written on the outside an apology then her name. None of his daughters knew the content of this room or why he came here. It was forbidden to talk about among the inhabitants of the castle. If you were not here years ago when the king was a child. Then you did not know what was behind this door. But even if you did not know what was behind the door, everyone knew not to approach it, or disturb him while he was there. Now for some reason his own daughter had broken that command.

King Charles had turned it over in his hand a few times, he weighed it and knew it was more than one page. What was this about? What could his daughter have possibly have written that she had to slide it under this door. He walked over to the bed with a curious look on his face then his eyes widened when an unpleasant thought struck him. He prayed that this was not a repeat of dreaded events played out by his own daughter, not because he now forced her to marry. Denied her to sit as his heir. He sat down and unfolded the letter.

'My dear father, my king. I beg pardon for the unpleasant contents of this letter. But it is very necessary that you become aware of this knowledge. I would be no daughter to you and a disgrace to with-hold this news to myself. A trader to the crown I would be. So, I impart to you the news I so terribly stumble upon these few days past. I ask that you do not think it a sly ploy of mine to have my way or to avoid being married. It is the truth as I am your daughter, undeniable. I have discovered that there is a plot to undermine your rule, to cheat in your tourney and at politics. A suitor has already been chosen for me by other than yourself. A ploy long ago set that will lead to the over throw of this kingdom. But it has been decided to enact only in part while you yet live. The brunt of it will fall on me and the kingdom lost.

Father, I happened upon a group of conspires whispering about cheating at the tourney and other things. This was followed by the angry whispered name of a lady named 'Princess Georgette'."

The king's heart skipped a beat at the sight of her name written. But Elizabeth does not know of her. How could she? He could no longer sit still and had no doubt that this was serious.

"This group swore that they should have done something about her a long time ago" he began to pace in front of the window. They believe the she is a threat to the crown. They believe that Jared is as well and that he should have been first to die, and that the lady that he is sent to find shall not enter the castle ever again. Caleb is to be hurt very badly by the end of the event or killed if necessary. I am to be wed to Prince Francis and upon you death the kingdom is to cede, join with the kingdom of Chamell. With them ruling over our people.

The king and queen of Chamell are in cahoots with Lord Gregory and his lady wife. There are other lords of your kingdom who will side with them. But; I most regrettably tell you that my mother, your lady Queen and wife is in on this ploy. Queen Juliah has laid this burden upon her before she passed'. King Charles did not like this at all. First his mother with his father, now his wife with him. His mother was dead and buried and yet she still held an influence on the kingdom. He was furious and almost crumpled the letter in his hand. He read the rest of it then folded it shoving it in his pocket.

They had planned to ruin his family. He would not suffer thus to be. King Charles scooped up his cub and left the room making sure the door was secure. This day was not to end pleasantly.

The guards seemed to have come from nowhere. The company was surprised to see them surround the lordling Caleb.

"Caleb, son of Lord John of Browning, you are summoned by the king". The lead guard stated.

"What is the meaning of this?" Lord John said rising from his seat.

"king's orders, and no-one is to follow or leave this room until further notice; orders of the king, King Charles."

The hall was in an up roar. No-one made a move to stop Caleb's escorts, or approach the exists of the hall. Two guards stood patrol by each exist and entrance.

In the east wing several guards marched on to the princess' room and banged loudly on the door. But waited not for an answer. They entered at the shocked squeals of young ladies and Princesses Elizabeth as well as princess Bethel stood surprised.

"Princess Elizabeth, you are summoned by the king, and not to delay. No-one is to leave this room. Guards will be posted." a guard told her. She allowed herself to be ushered away.

She thought about how she was to be punished for disturbing the king. She knew that she should not have listened to Caleb. That stupid boy set her up again.

Two groups of guards marched their wards along the halls unknown to each other, and they knew not where they were being led. When they met up and joined at the corner, Princess Elizabeth had attacked Caleb.

"I knew I should not have listened to you," she slapped him twice, "you stupid boy, I...oh" a guard picked her up and separated her from Caleb who stood shocked and holding his face. The guards began to carry the princess away but she demanded that they let go of her.

"Princess you must behave yourself, or we will be forced to bind your hands and carry you to the king."

"You will not." she said tightly.

"Yes we will, on the king's orders."

"Huh." was all she could manage to reply.

She was told to behave and follow the guard in front of her. Caleb felt a hand nudge him from behind. He was confused as to what this was about. What could they have done to deserve this treatment...? King's orders. The two of them were marched on to the southwest side. This was the side of the castle no-one hardly ever came. It was older and only ever used by the Royal Messengers when they were living in the castle. Of course the princess and Caleb had come here way before in their younger days as a challenge to each other. The auditorium was a lonely quiet place that seemed haunted by the long gone Royal Messengers. Cold and quiet. They could clearly and loudly hear their own footfalls as they walked on.

They came upon four guards, two posted on either side of the huge doors. A guard closest to the handle opened the door and bid Caleb and the Princess to enter. The Princess hesitated until Caleb walked past her. Caleb had thought that since he still carried his short sword they could not be in any serious trouble. As they entered, the door was closed behind them. Again this brought pause to the Princess' advance. She walked up behind Caleb and in her uncertainty grabbed his hand. He looked back at her and seen all the fearlessness gone from her face and continence.

"It cannot be that bad Elizabeth." he tried to reassure her.

"Look at this place. Caleb, you don't know."

"I'm still armed," he told her; "so it is not as bad as it may seems" he turned to her quietly and said, "did you do...did you go to, you know, earlier?"

She was confused at first then she caught on, "Yes, yes I did. That's when I saw Lady Chelsey coming from the rose garden. I was almost caught myself."

"Did anyone ask why you were over there?"

"No."

"Did Chads do it? Are you sure?"

"Yes. I stood there and watched him."

"Well then we should be alright."

"Do you think...?"

"No." he shook his head. "Let us move on. If the king summoned us then he is here somewhere. Come on." he led on as she never let go of his arm. Caleb had thought to draw his sword but did not wish to offend the king if this were his bidding. They made on slowly in what could have been a gathering hall. There were benches in two rows against the walls. Small tinted windows peppered the walls and in between were pitch torches. There were several outlets leading elsewhere and at the end or head, there was a door behind four high backed chairs. As the two made it to the middle of the hall they hear sounds which made the princess tighten her grip on Caleb's hand. The door behind the four chairs opened and the king's cub darted out from behind it and the king followed it. He did not look overly upset but still there was no smile on his face either. He walked up to them stopping just a few feet away and assessed them. He looked them over from head to toe. They were standing very close and holding hands. Actually it was the princess that was holding on to Caleb. For someone who didn't like his company she surely held on to him tight. She was frightened and held on to him for support. Caleb stood slightly in front of her and looked to be ready to draw his sword. The king did not show this to them but he was pleased at what he saw.

The king drew forth the letter and shoved it toward the Princess who flinched stepping further behind Caleb. "What is the meaning of this?" no-one spoke or moved, "Speak!" he raised his voice.

"Your Majesty, it is as the Princess explained." Caleb spoke up. He turned to the Princess and urged her to tell the king.

The king had never looked at her like this before. The seriousness of his voice and poise frightened her. But she seen that Caleb was not scared and he spoke for her. When was the Princess, the king's daughter; she had a duty to him. Nervously she said without stepping from behind Caleb. "I overheard them and thought it best that you know. But I did not know how to approach you with it. I did not want to disturb you but," she indicated to Caleb. "He told me to write a letter and give it to you right away."

"Do you swear that the contents of this letter is the truth, on your life?" the king asked.

"Yes." she replied softly and hesitantly.

Caleb spoke up again, "Your Majesty, I too put my life on it that the Princess has told you the truth."

"So you know of this matter?"

"Yes your majesty. I only caught so much when I happened upon the Princess. However, I do not know the Lady they spoke of. Also I do not believe that everyone is in on this. Such as the Bestles and Lord Jeffery are in the blind on this. I believe that Prince Conrad has discovered the truth and has accused his father of belittling his prowess and turning against his own son. But, King Gaston knew nothing of this. He almost struck the prince in public for his accusation. They went off to the side to speak of the issue. They may approach you soon, if not then I fear they will take leave. The Prince feels slighted.

"You two," the king pointed at the both of them. "Will carry on as if nothing is about." directly to Caleb he said. "You will inform your father and Lord Jeffery, they are to leave immediately and ready their men. I'm afraid there will be a civil war." he took a few steps away then turned back to them "Lord Robert has come to spy, this I Know. He will back Lord Gregory and King Perciville. I will speak to King Gaston and see to his aid. I will not suffer another challenge to my kingdom. I let them manipulate me before and keep my family apart." he paused and again spoke directly to Caleb. "Caleb, I will need you. Jared is not here, but I will try to wait for his return. I will not tolerate this."

"You know you can count on me Your majesty, I am at your service always." Caleb said. He felt the grip of the princess hand lighten. Her fear that they were in trouble had passed. But she still held his hand.

The king called for his cub and he scooped it up when it came happily to him. He told the two of them that they were dismissed. Caleb was to carry out his orders right away and lead on to no-one else anything. The tourney was to continue on as planned. If anyone was to ask, the king would say that he called the two because they were caught alone outside in the garden and accusations were made. They were to look shameful. King Charles would speak with King Gaston before the morrow. When the king dismissed them he wished he could call for Jared. The man was in way over his head and there were no more Royal Messengers to help him. Caleb would be the best to help him, but the king needed him here. This must come to an end, all those against him. With that thought the king felt a pain in his chest, for he truly love the queen dearly. He would not suffer treachery from within his own castle as his father did.

11

The guards had led the Princess back to her chambers and she held on to her embarrassed look. The guards posted at her door left when she returned. Neither said a thing. Caleb's guards took him back to the hall where he was and upon returning, his guards left as well. Caleb held the visage of a rebuked lad. He walked humbly to his father who stood looking at him. His eyes searching about him, "Caleb what is the matter? What was that about?"

"I, I am sorry father. I have been forbidden to approach the Princess during the remainder of our stay."

His mother approached, "Caleb, what have you done? Oh my." she turned to her husband "John what..."

"I must speak with father...alone" Caleb interrupted her.

Lord John looked none the happier. Had his son disgraced them so and in the presence of other nobles, and visiting kingdom's. "What is it you have to say?" he demanded of Caleb.

Before Caleb spoke, his eyes and the corner of his mouth twitched, his hand raised to touch his head but stopped. These slight actions brought a frown to Lord John's face. As he looked into his son's eyes, without letting on he knew what Caleb had done. His own hand raised to his mouth wiping down his chin.

"It must be alone." Caleb told him.

They had done this numerous times to let the other know that what they have to say cannot be said in public. Lord John bid Lady Carmen to relax and told her that he would be back in a moment. He turned and followed Caleb out of the hall. Caleb led him down a corridor to a small library where they took a room and closed the door behind them. Facing each other Lord John bid Caleb to speak.

"Father, it is not I that am in trouble, but the king himself." this widened Lord John's eyes. "There has been a treacherous ploy," Caleb continued. "For a long time between several nobles and the Chamell kingdom. I am afraid that our very own queen is involved as well."

Lord John was speechless and turned from his son. "You must not be serious." he said taking several steps away in the small room.

"Father I lie not to you on this matter. The princess and I happened upon a group of conspirators. They plan to have Jared killed and some Lady named Princess Georgette, who they think is a threat to their plans."

Lord John's jaw dropped "Princess Georgette, impossible." he said softly. "She had run away years ago. Oh, we all thought her to be dead."

"Father that is far from the truth." Caleb said shaking his head. "She was exiled by Queen Juliah. As it turns out the queen knew how much King George loved his daughter and thought that he would go against tradition and name her heir to his throne, over his son; Prince Charles. The queen and several nobles forced her to leave when the king became sick. They lied to him about her running away. They regretted that they let her live and promised to never let her step foot in the castle again. There was mention of them regretting Jared live when he was sent here. They think he is somehow a threat to the kingdom. The king knows that Lord Robert Loch is here as spy and against him. He will Back Lord Gregory and King Perciville will back them all. There will be a civil war and the king bids you to leave right away and ready your men. I am to stay here with mother as the tourney will continue in pretense. Lord Jeffery will be sent to ready his men as well. Without a scene you two are to leave right away. King Charles will speak with King Gaston about the aid of his men. I do not know what he has in mind for them to do."

"What of Brian?"

"He will be protected. Neither you nor Lord Jeffery are to take all the men you brought. That will cause too much attention. By the time the two of you leave and ready your men, the king's plan will be set into action. You will be instructed on what to do."

They stood there a moment searching for more words to say, something to part with. "I will be on my way." Lord John said. "You take care and be about your duties to the king, and your mother. I will see you on my return." he embraced him then with no further words, he left. Caleb went to speak with Lord Jeffery.

It was King Gaston that came upon King Charles. "I must speak with you Charles." he said heavily.

"Yes, I know and agree. I was about to search you out myself. Come with me, there are somethings that have been brought to my attention. Things that I do not like and will not suffer to happen." they both turned and walked off with King Charles slightly leading the way. "It is unfortunate that you have to hear of these deceptive ploys while visiting my kingdom. I feel embarrassed to not have seen any of these signs before-hand. Maybe I allowed myself to be blinded." King Charles led them outside to the square garden where they stood by the fount.

"Charles, what are you going to do about this?"

"It is broader then you think Gaston. It is more than a manipulation of my tourney." King Gaston had not heard anything more than the tourney scam and this showed on his face. King Charles knew he must tell him the rest. "Gaston, there is a ploy to overthrow my rule, subtly conquer my kingdom."

"What do you mean by this Charles? Speak to me."

"You are a visiting king in my kingdom and I consider you among my friends, so I must tell you Gaston. I have to give you an option. There will be a war here. I must fight to secure my rule and what I leave behind. I will declare this and the end of the tourney. But, Gaston; I ask that since you are here, will you stand beside me in battle?"

For a moment King Gaston did not know what to say. "Who are we to fight, Charles?"

"The Chamell's have sided with several of my nobles, or is it the other way around. Whatever the case, they wish to cede my kingdom to the Chamells. I am afraid that my Lady wife is with them."

"Charles no." Gaston said shaking his head. "Not Queen Alicene, she truly loves you Charles. You have to be mistaken. Who, who brought you this terrible news?"

"My daughter, Elizabeth caught them. I…" he was about to tell him that he too seen them but he was uncertain of the group he seemed so he kept it to himself. "She overheard their conversation. But the treason is not to be completed until after I'm dead. Weather by natural design or not. The kingdom will be taken from my heir."

They were both silence for some time, both lost in thought.

"Charles what will this cost me to stand with you hear. I barely have a hundred man with me." King Gaston told Charles.

"Just fifty of your fighters are ferocious, this we both know. But it is their archery that will serve me well. I do not wish you to lose your men in the heat of battle. But the arrows will do me justice. My battle here should not be long, but it will be viciously without mercy. Then I will move onto the Kingdom Chamell, but I must first straighten out my own home."

"Your people will help protect my ports and borders." King Gaston said as if for a fact. And if my Conrad is not successful with your Elizabeth, then your younger daughter will marry my Gentry. What do you say?"

King Charles smiled at that. "I assure you that my people will help protect your boarders, but your Gentry will have to prove himself to my Susan. That will be no easy task, she seems to favor your people's style of choosing a mate."

"That is more to my liking. We will sign an agreement and finalize this talk between us."

"It will be done. But Gaston, I do not wish any of the others to know of this until I am ready. I have sent two of my nobles to ready their men and by the time they get here, things will be in motion. You will know who they are by the days end. We will part now before there are any suspicious talk." They start to walk off than King Charles added. "Gaston you are my guest so I had to warn you of what I learned and what I plan to do about it. Still the choice is yours to do as you wish".

"I have decided to stand by you in this, but my people will only assist you as you suggested. I will have them informed. We wish you the best." Patting Charles in the back. "I will leave you now. I'm sorry that things turned out the way they did."

Charles knew that Gaston spoke of the treachery of his wife, more than troublesome nobles.

On the far side of the square Lord Robert stood at the edge of the window just out of view, He watched King Charles and Gaston until they parted. Now what was this about? Lord Robert knew something should had been done about this tourney charade of the kings. Charles did not understand all the benefits of joining with the Chamell. He did not realize how lenient he was and how eventually he would had lost his thrown and possibly his life. Lord Robert really thought that King Charles was not fit to rule. Too many things slipped passed his knowing. He may be the son of a king and a good fighter, but it takes more than a sport to keep a kingdom. Julia should had listen to him a long time ago and forced them to join with Chamell. Her son has many nobles against him and even his spies are not loyal to him. He shook his remembering the other older nobles thought he should had been vice Regent until they got a suitable king but he had enough to worry about with his own lands and people. Lord Robert thought that each Lord should take his own rule, making many smaller Kingdoms. Lord Robert now had the power to overthrow several Nobles and join their lands with his. He could truly benefit from this turn of events. But if he ever became a king he will show no mercy to those who oppose him. He turned from the window and headed back to his own chamber, he had to prepare his plans.

Unknown to Lord Robert, Lord John and Lord Jeffery had prepared their leave telling no one. He was here and his men chased Jared his plans will not go far at all. While he watched the kings talk, he did not see he too was being watched. He wouldn't even make it to learn of the tourney's end. He headed to his chamber were others awaited to apprehend him on king order's. He would not be happy to know what King Charles had plan for him.

12

Jared was well rested and ready to go on. He had left the shed of the generous man and his helpful daughter as the evening approached. He leaned heavily on his horse as it carried him away. Jared understood the man's concern for himself and his daughter, he did not want to bring unwanted attention upon them; so he left. Although he was able to get up, dress himself, mount his horse and rides off; he knew he would need more rest. He let his horse carry him for several hours guiding it along the edge of the forest into the night. When he thought it was a safe distance away from the man's place and it was well into the night, he slowly and carefully guided his horse in the forest looking for a sturdy tree with good solid limbs, a high tree. He came upon an oak, standing in his stirrups he climbed painfully up the tree to amidway distance and perched himself securely. He shooed his horse away then fell into a deep meditative slumber after he ate several of the smoked strips of meat the man gave him.

Jared slept undisturbed for the rest of the night and awoke at the approach of dawn. Simply by flexing and relaxing his muscles he allowed the blood to flow though his stiff limbs. He stretched then slowly climbed down from his perched spot. Jared walked for a good hour following the tracks of his horse but never left the safety of the forest. He found a clear spot that he could move around freely a few yards in each direction. He drew his long sword and holding it in two hands he pointed it at the ground. Jared took a deep breath and held it as long as he could. When he felt the strain of his lungs fighting for relief, he exhaled then quickly brought his sword up in an upward strike, stepping forward. His movements did not stop until he went through several attack moves. Thrust, chops, slashes of his long sword. He progressed in small steps, leaps, double steps, and short sprints. His arms began to burn with the weight of his long sword and non-stop movements. The muscles in his legs tightened and sweat began to spot his forehead, nose and upper lip. His hair lay limp down his back. He switched from is long sword to is short sword then daggers. He went through several attack moves then defense moves. Jared loosened his cape and dropping his weapons went through hand and feet routines. The sun was two hours in the sky before he stopped.

Jared's trusty horse found him as he waited at the edge of the forest. He believed he was ready to go on and left the forest behind. He mounted his horse and rode off at a slow canter. He could sense the eagerness in his horse to run hard and fast, so he tightened his knees and let his horse have its way. They rode hard into a town and passed surprised people. Some of the younger kids ran behind him for a while until they tired or felt they ran far enough from their homes. The farther his horse ran, the longer they went on, Jared felt more like himself. He tried not to think about the last attack but it kept slipping into his thoughts. He was very close to death. There was enough strong poison in that dried meat to render him immobile and unconscious for hours. His horse dragging him to the man's place most likely saved his life. His body could have fought off the poison by itself, but it would have taken at least a whole day to be rid of it. His strength to move would have been slower as well. If his attackers were anywhere around he would have been finished off easily. He had no way to defend himself. Suddenly he was struck with another thought, was this how they got to the other Royal messengers. Had they poisoned them first then killed them in their defenseless state? He did not like the thought of that at all. He did not mind dying in a fight, even if the odds were against him. But rendering him defenseless, immobile that was a cowardice slaughter and unfit for a Royal Messenger to die that way.

The day moved on into evening then night. He brought his horse to a gallop but continued on into the night. The moon was bright and clear of any clouds. He decided to go on until the moon moved on itself. He needed to make up time and since no-one was hindering his path, he went on. He came across another river and rode its edge allowing the water to cool his heated horse. Before the river turned off on another course he stopped to drink. Both he and the horse drank deep then he walked for half an hour resting his horse and his own rump.

Thoughts weighed heavy on his mind as he climbed back on his horse. Who was this lady he sought? The mere sight of the sky blue letters brought tears to the king's eyes and hatred from some of the nobles. But what worried him the most was what the king would not tell him. What had this lady had to do with him? Why had the king embraced him so? As a child Jared had been protected by the king, he slept in the same chambers and all his food was tasted before he could eat. The king had treated Jared as he would a son. At least until his training began. Then, he seen less and less of the king until his training was complete. After that the king treated him not like a son, but as any other Royal Messenger. He barely had time to talk to him and any question he asked of his past was brushed off. It seemed as if everyone had been forbidden to talk about him. It wasn't his past, it was his origin, his parents, or if he had any siblings or other relatives somewhere, anywhere. It wasn't until all the Royal Messenger were released, except him, the king showed any further interest in him. The king would not release him from his oath, duty, or sight. He had argued and yelled at the nobles who tried to point out that Jared too was a Royal Messenger and must be let go. The decision counted him in as well but the king would have none of it. For some time guards were posted around Jared's chamber and followed him around wherever he went. The king threatened to punish anyone who tried to harm him or even speak of his departure from the castle. Several times Jared caught the king watching him from afar. Other times he would approach him as if to tell him something, but then change his mind.

Jared had free reign of the castle and was the only one who could be around the king well-armed at any time (besides his personal guards). But there was only three people that would approach Jared at any given time freely. The king being one and then the two princesses being the others. Their relationship was like siblings and they loved Jared and treated him as an older brother. Then there was the rumor about him being the king's son. Which was about the same time the king was accused of fathering Caleb as well. Caleb was another one that would approach Jared freely, even though he did not live in the castle. Caleb adored him growing up and even learned how to fight from him. But still, none of them knew where he came from. Now, the king tells him that the lady he sought and was to bring back would tell him all. This made him anxious and nervous at the same time. He would finally find out who he was, who his parents are. He had to find this lady who was on her death bed. This made the matter all the more important, to himself. He needed to know these things, wanted to desperately to know them. He must find her and if anyone tried to stop him, he would show no mercy. He vowed this to himself and meant to keep it.

The moon had made its course and now was gone from the sky. The stars began to wink out of sight and the dawn was fast approaching. When the sun began to rise Jared squeezed on his horses flanks and she picked up her pace until she ran fast and hard. Jared came upon another town and meant to be though it as fast as his horse could run.

It was now noon as he passed the huddled homes and approached a spacious meadow. An arrow struck the vest of his horse but fell away. His first thought was to dig in the flank and press on but instead he jumped from the horse into a running sprint and followed behind her with his daggers drawn. From the high grass in which he now ran, arrows shot toward him from several angles, however; all in front of him. He swatted them away as he watched some of them strike at his horse and fall away. Her vest was tough and designed for this. She ran on unscatched. The further he ran into the meadow it was easier to see his foes pop up from their hiding places. He threw his daggers, each one hitting their intended mark. Drawing his short sword, Jared wanted to be up close on his foes and the long sword would not do. As he ran on his cape bellowed out and his braid swayed cross his back. He met his first foe with clenched teeth and clanging word. Jared had no intention of entertaining them in a fight, he meant to slaughter them all out right. He snatched his sword back and kicked out, snapping the first man's knee. It broke with a snap and the man screamed out and crumbled to the ground. Jared's sword impaled him and lifted him back up. He fell backward into one of his own men. Jared snatched the sword free. A slash to the waist then high to the neck brought another one down. He twisted away from one man and stepped right into the path of another. His sword parried hard blows from this man, but a quick ducking drop and thrust of his left hand Jared cut deep into the man's upper thigh at the corner of his groin with his wrist blade. He pushed the man away and still in his low position kicked out and up at the man he twisted away from.

Their number and close attacks made Jared stay alert. Their skills were not impressive and in ten minutes twelve men were dead. One was stomped to death by his horse. Before he moved on he retrieved his weapons and made sure all the men were dead. If Jared gad any thought that this was the first and last for the day, he was proven wrong. Every hour and a half to two, he was attacked by a group of ten to fifteen men. The attacks were always the same, they started out with arrows at first then when he was upon them they drew swords. And of course the outcome was always the same, ending with Jared checking to make sure all were dead, then retrieving his weapons before he moved on.

Jared grew tired of these distraction but he pressed on. He had to travel this route. The way things were going he would have at least two days travel to get to the town of Woodberry, where the lady was to be. Then he still had to search her out.

The attacks stopped and the night came on, but Jared kept a careful watch throughout. Nothing else occurred. At the break of dawn Jared ate the last of his smoked meat and bread the man gave him. He led his horse into some barn and feed her there from their supplies. The tenet had come out in an uproar, alerted by the dogs barking. Upon seeing the Royal Messenger the man apologized and backed off. Jared stayed long enough to feed his horse and bathe. The sight of his uniform was enough for most people, he did not want splattered blood all over him to intensify the effects. With his uniform still wet, he left the barn on his horse at a full out run.

This day Jared rode on undisturbed and tried to make up for any lost time. He raced on the whole of the day and well into the night guided by the moon's light. He slowed towards midnight so that his horse would rest and not stumble or be surprised by anything in the night. Unhindered he made it through the night.

13

Again the breakfast table was crowded with food as if this was a feastful morning. Everyone shambled down to the dining hall making their unusual small talk and morning greetings. The seats were full except for four chairs. There was questioning looks here and there but no-one actually made any suggestions or reasons why. Shortly after they were all seated, King Charles joined them. They made to stand but he waved them not to do so. It had been two days since he joined their company. He appeared as if nothing ever happened nor was amiss. He didn't even let on that he noticed the empty hairs.

There were Lords missing from their group. Lord John was absent and it was plain that Lady Carmen did not know the reason why. She kept looking at Caleb for some time hoping that he would give her something, some type of answer. But he only shrugged his shoulders as if he knew nothing. The lordling Brian sat alone without his father next to him, and he to revealed nothing. As for Lord Robert, everyone knew that he was unpredictable and would come and go as he pleased.

When the king sat he ate hungrily for a moment without pause. He then told everyone that the tourney would pike up after the noon meal. Faces were alighted but there were still questions behind the smiles. King Charles was the first to leave the table, then all followed suit excusing themselves for different reasons. Lady Carmen lingered around and waited on Caleb to leave the table. She caught hold of him to slow him.

"Caleb, what is going on? Where is your father?" there was concern in her voice but also command in her words.

"Mother, I don't know where father is and I don't know what you mean by what is going on. Is there something that I should know about?" he asked his mother with a curious look about him.

"Well, I just assumed that you would know. You spoke to him yesterday after the king sent you back. So I..."

"Mother, if something is going on or amiss, I don't know about it. I'm quite sure he'll turn up somewhere soon."

"But Caleb, your father has near just..."

"Don't worry about it mother. Father is a capable man he can take care of himself. Wherever he is for whatever reason, he must have felt it necessary to not mention it to us. Don't worry, he'll be alright."

Lady Carmen didn't like any of Caleb's excuses to avoid her. She knew that he knew something, but also that it was worthless to carry on about it. She would get nowhere or nothing out of her son. She let it go. "Well," she said letting go of the anxiousness, or at least trying to. "What do you have planned for the noon?"

"I have none."

"Then you wouldn't mind going for a walk, would you?"

"I would enjoy it." he said extending his arm to her and she accepted as a proud mother would.

The noon meal came and gone, and the same empty chairs were still empty. Dressed as dazzling as thy might, all the guest made it to their designated seats for the tourney to resume. Two of the chairs were empty. Lord Robert had never taken a chair among them. The events were set off nicely and without delay. The competition was heavy among the suitors. There were many events, gavilan, archery, fencing and hand to hand combat. In between these physical activities by the King's allowance, the Princess asked questions to her liking. All the suitors had visited her on several occasions and should have known something about her. Things she liked or did not like. She asked questions about politics and had put each one to question as if they had to sit as judges to case brought by their subjects. The mothers of the suitors actually liked this and encouraged the princess to ask certain questions. There was even a small chess tournament. They had to think quickly in the game but win by saving the most pieces, no-one could just play a trade out game.

The tourney went on well into the night and by its end there were only three suitors left. Gregory the iii and Brian were out. It was down to Prince Conrad, Prince Francis, and Caleb. Prince Francis did not look to be doing too well against the others. Then suddenly Prince Conrad was outed. There were several puzzled faces throughout the night. Glances snatched here and there with eyebrows raised in question. The king called it a day with Prince Francis and the lordling Caleb. They would continue on the morrow and by days end, the Princess Elizabeth will have a fiance.

Much later that night in the same place as the last time a group huddled in together. This time there group consisted of only women. Queen Alicene, Queen Audrey, and Lady Chelsey. Queen Audrey was the last to join the group.

"What the hell is going on here, Alicene" she demanded.

"Hush, lower your voice." Alicene whispered.

"It was not supposed to turn out like this. I want to know what is going on." Audrey said.

"I don't know any more than you do." Alicene replied.

"Francis is not supposed to be left challenging that Caleb. Caleb is not even supposed to still be in this farce of a competition."

"I know, or so we agreed."

"I thought that you had put that spell on him?" Lady Audrey asked.

"It was, and Francis did all that he was supposed to do." Audrey said "Something had to go wrong."

"Well that is the obvious Audrey, but what?" Alicene asked.

"Could, could he have a counter spell...to...you know to block all the magic? Something to prevent someone from casting on him?" Chelsey asked.

"Nothing is impossible. But why would he have such a thing here? This is not a deathly battle, who would think that any of the suitors would have magic intervention at an engagement tourney?" asked Alicene.

"You are right, Alicene. It would be seen as cheating and cause for a real fight." Chelsey put in.

"Exactly. But, no allegations have been brought forth. So what do you assume, Audrey"?

"I don't know, but I know something is not right." she wanted to turn away in frustration but did not want to lose her composure. "Ever since that Caleb was summoned by Charles I knew something was amiss." Audrey said.

"But what? Besides Francis' magic not working, what could it be?" Alicene asked.

"I don't know, but tell me this. Where is Lord John and Lord Jeffery? Even that meddling Lord Robert is missing. They, all three go missing after Caleb, and the Princess; if it be true, were summoned by the King. Then all of the sudden Charles shows back up as if he were never gone. Caleb remains the last challenger when he should have been the first one outed." Audrey's look was suspicious on Alicene and she caught it.

"What are you implying, Audrey?"

Audrey ignored the question. "Have you spoken with Beatirce?"

No. she will have none of our politics. She worries about her own among her own people back home and leaves foreign politics to her husband and son. She will not join us. But, you still avoid my question. Are you implying that I..."

"No, no. I just..."

"You have worked no harder at this than I have. It was imparted to me to make sure that our kingdoms were joined. Juliah had this in the works with your husband's people before you or I came along. She has put this upon my shoulders and I have not been negligent in my part. Remember it is my kingdom that will be ceding to yours, not the other way around. I have crossed my husband and daughter for this." she did turn away feeling a little guilt creep up on her as she spoke.

"I know Alicene, I am sorry. I just don't know what could have went wrong. Audrey said.

"That damn Jared and Georgette, that's what went wrong." Alicene turned back. Her guilt gone now hinted on anger. "Why did she have to wait until now to come back into the picture? Of all times, why now?"

"Everyone knows that Charles won't portray anything dealing with Jared and we all know how he feels about Georgette. Neither topic is open for discussion with him." Chelsey put in.

"That Lord Robert didn't just pop up for nothing. He sure as hell couldn't care less who Elizabeth married. We all know that he came because of Georgette and her damned letters. He will not suffer her to come back here. He will try to stop Jared from seeking her out or reaching her." Audrey said.

Lady Chelsey as nervous as the others but somehow they managed to stay still while she pranced from foot to foot like a nervous horse. "Have you seen how Lady Carmen has been acting all day?" she finally stopped and said to them all.

"Yes I have." Alicene answered "Her son was summoned and escorted to the King like a criminal. He was caught with Elizabeth when they should not have been alone. And now her husband is missing. She is scared and uncertain."

"I too have seen that." Audrey put in. "But have you noticed Caleb? He acts as if nothing is wrong. He is behind something and Elizabeth knows it. Charles may be carrying on as normal, but that Caleb and Elizabeth; those two are not."

Chelsey looked up as if she remembered something she should have not forgotten. "I seen her the other day."

"What do you mean you seen her the other day? We see each other every day." Alicene said.

"No, no. when you told me of the rose garden. I went, but when I was coming out I seen her coming from the left corridor. She approached me with some questions but Gregory came around the corner. She, she stopped whatever she was about."

"But there is nothing over there. The rose garden is the last place anyone goes in that area. Beyond that is the..." Alicene's brow frowned. She shook her head not wanting to believe what she was thinking.

"What is beyond the rose garden, Alicene?" Audrey asked

She looked up, "The sorcerer Chad's quarters. She said.

"Why would she be over there? What dealings could she have with a sorcerer?" Chelsy asked.

Alicene shook her head. Now she began to pace. Speaking more to herself, but aloud. "But she doesn't even like Caleb. My daughter has never liked him."

"Could it be a ruse? Alicene, do you know for a fact that those two are not playing games with us? They could be in cahoots." Chelsey said

"I don't like the way this is turning out. Alicene you need to get to the bottom of this before the tourney ends." Audrey said with authority.

"I will speak with Francis and tell him to try again. Caleb cannot win the princess' hand that would ruin everything we worked so hard for. You have a lot more to lose than we do." she said to Alicenen then looked to Chelsey "or maybe just me. Both of you will have a lot to answer for if Caleb becomes heir to the throne. We all know he will not cede to us. And if Jared survives...." she took several steps away then turned back. "All hell is going to break loose with those two... and Charles." her words seemed more of a demand than just statements. She seemed not too happy at all and charged Alicene with the obligation to fix the mess as if she were the one to blame.

"I will find out what I can, but we need to prepare for the worst. We need to find a way past Caleb, if by chance he wins." Alicene said.

"I will consult with Gregory on this." Chelsey said

"And I with Perciville. He will not be happy about this." said Audrey's

"None of us will be. But we will do as we must." Alicene told them.

"Then we must depart. Tomorrow, there is more tourney then celebration. We are all expected." Audrey said. Without waiting a response she turned and left them. The two other women went their own way afterwards.

Only a few minutes had passed then two figures had quietly stepped out of the bushes where they were hiding. "I am sorry father, but I thought you might not believe me." Princess Elizabeth said

"I did not doubt your words, but... seeing this is something more hurtful." King Charles replied.

"I don't..."

"It is not your fault, Elizabeth. I will deal with it accordingly. Lord Robert has already been apprehended and confined. I have sent the two lords off to prepare. You will continue on as normal. But when my forces are ready to depart, it will be you I leave behind; so guard yourself. Elizabeth I need no childish, wishful taunts or demands from you. You are not a child anymore and when I depart you will be in my stead. Caleb will be with me, at my side. Your mother…," he paused for the pain was evident. "…your mother will not be a problem. But, there may be others that will try to influence you."

"I know father. Jared has told me of them all. I do pay attention to you and him when you speak. I know how to run and control this castle I your stead. I will simply do as you do, or would do. I will not fail you…, or Caleb."

It surprised her that she would include Caleb, but her father only smiled. "You have to get some rest now. Tomorrow will be a busy day. I am sorry it will come to this."

"Me to father. I would have never guessed that mother was a part of this."

"Well, there is nothing to change it now. You go on ahead now."

King Charles kissed her on the forehead then led her through a hidden doorway in the side wall. The same they came through so that on-one would ever know that they had come and gone. This door was not known to many and its use had been stopped long ago. Only the two servants that maintained the rose garden ever came this way here on a regular basis and not even they know about this door. King Charles lead her along the wall corridor bringing her to her own hall way. She left the inside passage and went on to her own chambers. She lay down with a heavy heart. How could her mother do this? She was a mother and a queen, yet she made a choice to turn against her own daughter. That is what struck her the most. Elizabeth understood politics and people being placed in certain positions, playing roles here and there; doing their part. She knew that it wasn't rare for a wife to turn on her husband. But a mother turning on her own offspring. Who would go that far and for what reason? What had her father and or grandfather done that her mother thought to bring down their kingdom, to plot against them? She prayed that she would never be confronted with something like that.

14

The morning of the final day of the tourney had arrived. Even the suitors and their parents who were no longer in the tourney were eager to see this day come. The outcome of who would engage the Princess Elizabeth would affect them all. For they all had some type of dealings with this kingdom. Who would succeed King Charles would be a great deal to them because that's who they will eventually have to deal with. They all had their next to finest clothes out and ready to adorn. Their finest was set aside for the engagement party.

When the morning meal was announced the chairs were emptier than they usually were. Lord John, Lord Jeffery and Lord Robert had still not shown up. But this morning neither King Charles nor Princess Elizabeth showed up with the rest. They all ate in silence, which did not last long. The hall doors banged opened and a group of guards rushed in surrounding the royals who sat at the table. They were in an uproar and looked around in shock and wonder. The uproar was silenced by two guards who escorted in a lone robed middle aged man. Several eyes widened with shocked horror. Lady Chelsey fainted in her chair. King Charles and Princess Elizabeth came in together and neither had a smile on their face. King Charles' voice rang out, "The tourney is no more! This man before you is Stephen, he is a sorcerer in the employ of Lord Gregory and by his own confession was sent to give Prince Francis a spell to interfere with the suitor Caleb. He was not the only one that was hindered." whispers raced around the table and Lord Gregory made to stand and defend against the accusations. A guard forced him to sit. King Charles continued on. "Lord Gregory, Lady Chelsey, King Perciville and Queen Audrey, Lord Robert," he paused "and Queen Alicene. They all have conspired in cahoots against me to overthrow my kingdom, force it to cede to the Chemell's. Treason!" Even the servants trembled at that shouted word. "They were all witnessed to their plots by the Princess Elizabeth and young Lord Caleb (that was a first for the address) these here days past." Anger and disappointment was evident in the king's voice. "But in the midnight, I, myself witnessed with the Princess by my side to Lady Chelsey and the two queens in their plotting while in the rose garden. It is nothing new that they have started. Them, and their people are against me. They have plotted the demise of my sister, Princess Georgette during my father's rule. They have plotted to kill her first born, and all here know him as my Royal Messenger Jared. He is my sister's child and my nephew." The surrounded group continued to be amazed. Eyes looked around and mouths hung open in surprise to this revelation. "I will not suffer anymore tournament to my family. You have forced me into silence at first, and I had to succumb to you. But now you still plot against me. No more! You force my hand to war." King Charles stepped up to the table pointing. "Queen Alicene, you are under arrest. Guards constrain her."

Queen Alicene tried to shake the guard's hand off her but their grip tightened. Princess Susan and Lady Mary had tears in their eyes. Lord Gregory was just as silent as his wife and son, King Perciville and Queen Audrey along with their son Prince Francis had looks of defiance on their faces. The youngest son sat in shock.

"As for the rest of you," King Charles said looking around the table at the guilty parties. "I will give your people a chance to prepare for my coming. You will be escorted to your belongings and you will leave this day. Lord Gregory, you will have two weeks to return home and prepare your people. I am coming and will show no mercy. King Perciville Fontz, you will have two weeks longer than him. When I am done with my own home, I will come to yours. You and I will see whose land and people will dominate. You want my land so bad, I now give you your chance. But it will be on equal footing." King Charles walked up to him, "You think that I should not be king, that I should not have this reign you will have your chance to prove it. Guards!" They had approached all those that the King has named. They were encircled and escorted out of the hall.

When the guards had escorted those away, King Charles told the one holding the Queen Alicene to take her to the dungeon. She was not to be approached by anyone without his permission. The sorcerer was taken away as well. When they were all gone King Charles seemed to deflate. He walked to his chair and sat down heavily.

"I am very sorry about the turn of events," he said to the remaining "if you wish to leave, I will not stop you. I do wish to tell you that Caleb, if he agrees to accept; has been chosen as the Princess' fiance. They are to be considered engaged." King Charles faced Caleb who in turn nodded his head.

"Thank you your Majesty. I accept." he said

King Charles picked through the plate of bacon, he took several strips and ate them. "Lord Jeffery and Lord John have been sent to ready their men already. Brian, you have a choice to remain here or return home. Likewise to yourself Lady Carmen. King Gaston and I have already spoken and I will not discuss our conversation." he was silent for a while and helped himself to a bigger plate of food.

Lord Gregory and his family were escorted to their rooms by the guards and there awaited them their servants that came with them. They were told that all of their men were rendered weaponless. The majority of their belonging were already packed by the servants so there wasn't much for them to do. Gregory the 111 watched his parents in silence as they bickered back and forth about whose fault it was that they were discovered, why their plans hadn't worked and who would be the best men to lead them into battle against the King's men. Who or how many would turn against them for the King. They had not paid attention to their son since they left the dining hall. He was truly disgusted with them and their ever scheming failures.

"Did either of you think that you would live forever?" he asked them raising his voice above their chattering. They stopped and looked at him. It was as if they didn't even know he was present with them. "You plot and plan as if you won't die and leave this place behind. As if no-one is to succeed you. Have stopped to think what the outcome would be for me. What if things went wrong?"

"Your life has been chosen and prepared for you, boy." Lord Gregory told him

"Really father? A life you just forfeited. I have no life now because of you two."

"Now you complain?" Lord Gregory said going to his son. "You said nothing when you thought you could engage the Princess."

"Because it was my doing. It had nothing to do with fighting the King. Nothing to do with forfeiting my life!" he stood face to face with his father.

"Your father did what he thought was right, and best for us all." Lady Chelsey said coming over to stand next to them. She placed a hand on her husband's arm.

"You have no right to say what is best."

"Gregory." she said as if surprised by his words.

"No. He was following your crazy father's footsteps. Trying to please you. You wanted this, not him."

"Gregory, you will not speak to your mother like this." Lord Gregory said pointing a finger at his son.

"You are right. I will not speak to her, or you ever again." He shoved past his father and strode to the door where the guards blocked his exit. "Get out of my way!" he told the guard, but none of them moved.

"You will all be escorted to your carriage together, when all of your belongings are packed." The guard told him.

Gregory the 111 felt trapped, suffocated; he wanted to strike out at the guard but knew that would not be wise. His mother looked at him on the verge of tears. She looked from her husband to her son. Was this really all her fault. Had she really doomed her husband and son by following behind her father's idea. It was too late for those thoughts. They could take nothing back, and Lord Gregory was not a man to apologize for his actions, no matter the reason. Their course was set, they would head home and prepare for war. They would rally their allies, for they had quite a few. She knew her husband, they would not just surrender at the announcement of war. It was more than just her house that shared the idea as to who should be in rule over them. The Chamelle kingdom was just as large as theirs, but older. Lady Chelsey and the other nobles like her thought that the Chamelle governing was better, more stern, and better implemented than King Charles or his father.

On second thought, Lady Chelsey was not upset that it came to this, she just thought it was unfair at how unprepared they were. They were caught off guard. They had all thought that Charles' reign would come to an end without bloodshed. She didn't like blood, but didn't like being wrong even more. Being caught and cornered kept her nervous and it showed easily.

Their belongings were packed and ready. They were escorted as one out of the castle to their carriage. Neither Lord Gregory nor their son said a word to each other. Gregory the 111 rode in a separate carriage than his parents. All of those that came with them were stripped of their weapons and waited for them to come out. King Charles had forbidden and taken their banner so that it would not be raised with theirs. Their escort would lead them to the first town away from the castle and then all their weapons would be returned to them.

King Charles, his two daughters, and Caleb stood on the balcony overlooking the drawbridge and watched as they left. The mood was total opposite as from when they came and due to their escort, their procession seemed larger leaving than when it came. Only footfalls from men and horses could be heard above the sound of the carriage wheels.

Almost an hour after the Beal nobles had departed, King Charles and Caleb watched from the same balcony the Fontz leave. Prince Federick had the most disappointing facade the king had ever seen upon him. The boy had no idea what his parents or older brother was up to. It was clear that he wanted no part of it either. King Charles hung his head at the sight of him.

The boy's fate was already sealed and he hadn't even had the chance to live or enjoy his life. It was unfair, the fate of a child was set, decided by his parents unthoughtfulness of the child's well being and future. "Selfish parents." King Charles stated openly. He had thought of his earlier statement that he would show no mercy and he meant to keep his word. He watched the Fontz cross the drawbridge and didn't like what he would have to do.

Lord Robert had been the first to leave the day before, just as quietly as he came. So now all the expected warring party heads were gone. The lordling Brian had left before the Beals, to be with his father in readying their men. Lady Carmen and Mary had choose to stay at the castle until they heard from Lord John. Their son Harry would return to Brownsin while Lord John and Caleb fought in the coming wars. A Clemons male was needed to be there to ensure that Lord John's line would have an heir to succeed him, just in case the worst happened.

King Charles faced Caleb. "Well now, we have faced down two battles against the Starkens and won each. This will not be the same, Caleb. You will be fighting against many people who you know, who once fought beside you. It will not be easy but it must be done. Do you have the stomach for this?"

"Your majesty, I have the stomach to do what is right." his look was determined. "Justice is how we do things your majesty, not emotionally. War is never a pretty thing, and just because it must be done; it does not mean that we have to like it. I believe it was you, your majesty that told me that before."

"Saying it is easier than doing it. Will you be able to draw your sword on your fellow countrymen?"

Caleb was silent as he looked at the king. He took a deep breath, "Your Majesty, I understand your pain and indecision. You face a great problem in front of you. I believe what pains you the most is what you will have to do with the queen. You love her, but it is true that she betrayed you. She made a decision to betray you and her children, her children's future. Justice will secure your kingdom your Majesty, not emotion."

"You will make a fine king, Caleb." King Charles smiled and placed a hand on Caleb's shoulder. "If you don't let women folk control you. Come on, we must prepare for battle."

They left the balcony and headed to the barrack where they found King Gaston and Prince Conrad. They decided to call in his men from the docks to join them. The king's general was instructing him on where his men would be stationed with their arrows. This was the only part that King Gaston's men were to take part in. He stayed on to hear the rest of the arrangement and didn't hesitate to voice his opinion.

Queen Beatrice was left with the princesses. Elizabeth and Bethel were fine and coping well, but Susan was distraught. Her mother had betrayed her father and was now stuck in a dungeon, allowed no visitors. Her father was preparing for war with their own people and then the Fontz. She would not be able to see her father for a while. Her mother will be tried for treason, but will her father actually kill her. She was in an emotional shamble. Her friend Lady Mary tried to console her but that only went so far. She knew that Lady Mary would be leaving soon.

Everyone else in the castle tried to busy themselves and not speak out loud much about what was seen or heard in the dining hall, or how the Queen was practically dragged to the dungeon by escort without grace. The special events and celebration for the day turned sour leaving nothing to celebrate this day.

15

In the late afternoon Jared reached the town of Woodberry. He walked his horse along in the town and as always he received the same reaction from the people. They shunned him like the plague. Those that talked to him had no choice, he had them cornered. As always you had the curious children that seen his huge horse and thought that he was dressed really neat. They had never seen anyone dressed like him before and of course, they knew nothing of him or what he was.

Jared walked along and asked his questions about the lady who traveled with a young man with long black hair. The lady favored the color sky blue. Many people denied seeing her and some said they have but knew not where she stayed. They said she came and went as she wished and never saying where she came from or where she was going. Of all those that spoke of her, no-one said anything bad about her or the young man she traveled with.

Jared paid for a rod for fishing and paid a farmer to allow his horse to be fed and washed. Even though he was not approached by anyone suspicious, it was evident that he was being watched by not so friendly eyes. Several times he spotted men in plain clothes that were not your everyday farmers or town's people. These men, their gait and stance was of a trained or conditioned man, a soldier or guard. They watched him and he watched out for them. As the night came on Jared continued his walk and search. The town of Woodberry had a slim river and was spotted with ponds and small lakes. It was well populated and the ground good for farming. Lord Kenneth held this town and Jared knew him to be just in his governing. Lord Kenneth was for the kingdom of Stradin and its best interest against foreigners. To him, it did not matter who was king.

Lord Kenneth's land was on the boarder of the kingdom closest to the Starkens boarder and yet only separate from the king's castle land by a strip of land a complete two days ride. This was land governed by Lord Vincent. Of all the nobles, only Lord Robert Loch and Lord Vincent Markle were older than Lord Kenneth. Lord Brian of Lakewood had just passed leaving Lady Carol a widow, she was lord Kenneth's age but but her son Carlton now Lorded over the Lakewood lands.

Jared had already eaten several fish he caught and his horse was well taken care of. The night clouds had blocked the moon's brightness so Jared decided to rest for the night. He was already in the town he needed to be in and only had to find the lady he sought. He had picked a big tree to lean against as he sat down to relax for the night. He allowed his horse to roam freely.

Shortly after he sat down he saw a small hooded figure running about from shadow to shadow, trying to stay out of clear sight. The figure ran hunched over making sure it was clear from spot to spot before it moved on. The closer it got to Jared, its intention was clear that it meant for Jared only to see it. When it was a few yards away it stopped behind a tree and called to Jared in a whispered voice.

"Pst, hey Royal messenger sir, pst." it was the voice of a child. Jared gestured for the child to come closer but it refused. "My mother bids you to come in, this night is not good to be out. My mother knows these things sir." the child looked about. "She said she knows the two of whom you speak of and seek. The night is not a good night to be out, you should come inside." Jared stood and bid the child to lead the way.

The child led the way running from spot to spot. Jared on the other hand walked openly, but at a safe distance as if he were not following the child. His horse seeing him, got up and followed. They had walked a good five minutes when Jared's head began to tingle. Someone was using magic on him. A searching spell. He could tell that someone was looking for him. He continued to follow the child until it disappeared behind a shed. Jared stood still for a while and waited. The child came back with an older lady, they both gestured for him to come on and hurry up. Jared grabbed the reigns of his horse and walked to where they were standing. The lady, Jared thought was most likely the child's mother. She ushered them in the shed.

"Your horse will be fine in here." she said, "Come on, follow me." she lead Jared to the other side of the shed and out a short distance to another building. As soon as Jared stepped outside of the shed he could feel the searching spell again in his head. It went away when they stepped inside the lady's home. The child shut the door behind them and Jared chanced a question.

"You have this place, your home guarded?"

The lady looked out the windows before she answered him. "You mean from magic? Yes, yes. How can you tell?" she asked facing him.

"When I was outside, I felt the spell." Jared looked around the place. "But when I stepped in your shed it went away. Then the same thing coming in here."

The child removed its hood and stood next to its mother. The boy was quite young. "I keep this place guarded for my friends. They come here often enough, and they too are often sought after".

"And who would be these friends, if you don't mind"? Jared asked her.

"The same that you seek. Come sit down. Jacob will get you some water". The child went off and Jared followed the lad to the kitchen area of her home. No sooner than they sat down they heard the thunderous sound of mounted horses. The lady looked at him. "The same who search for you".

"What of the child"?

"He did not go far, he will be alright".

Jared looked in the direction the boy ran off in then back to the lady. "Why did you assist me? You know..."?

"Yes, yes I know who you are, Jared". The lady said surprising him. Many people outside the castle knew what he was, but none knew his name. He had always been addressed by his title. "I was told to expect you. You came sooner than I thought you would".

Jared did not know what to expect. He didn't sense any danger or threat from the lady, but he still did not fully relax in his seat. The boy returned with a pail of water and the lay went to get some cups. She filled a cup and handed it to Jared. She did the same for herself. He accepted and drank the cold water.

"My friend is old now and can no-longer move about as she once had. She does not fair well and fears dying". She looked Jared over from he sat. "Since I have known her, she has had many wondering questions about you".

"Questions of me? Why so?"

"You will meet her tomorrow." the lady said smiling. "She will tell you herself. You are safe here for tonight. I have had a long day and I tire. Tomorrow I will tell you how to find her. Jacob will get you some blankets to lay on, if you wish." she rose nudging the child on. "Until the morrow, Jared." she walked off into another room of her not so big house, leaving Jared sitting in the kitchen area. The child came out and lay a few blankets on the floor by the wall where the lady went into. The last blanket Jacob laid out was sky blue, then he disappeared into the room as well.

Jared walked over to the pile 0f blankets and picked up the last one, the sky blue one. It was the same color as the letters he delivered to the king. The same as he carried. He picked the blanket up and could smell the perfume on it as he held it in his hands. It was a sweet fragrance. Jared sat down on the blankets and held the sky blue one as he thought of who the lady could be. How did she know his name? Of all the people in the king's service, why was he sent for? What did the lady know of him? His thoughts carried him into a light slumber. He woke twice in the night to the sound of running horses.

Before the sun rose or the cock crowed, Jared woke to a light nudging at his leg. He woke to the lady standing off to the side with a long stick in her hand. He looked from her to the stick.

"I did not know how you would react to someone standing over you, or touching you while you slept." she too looked at the stick, "I prefer safer than sorry. But, I do apologize if I offended you."

"Do not worry, I understand". He said getting up from the floor. He had fallen asleep sitting up with his legs stretch out.

"Come, if you wish to reach my lady friend by noon; you should head out now. You have many hours yet before you can reach her, and I cannot come with you." she walked Jared to the shed where his horse stayed the night. She instructed him on how to get to where he needed to go. She gave him some dry meat and bread, and several pieces of cheese. The cheese was a gift that the lady would bring her. Jared thanked her and left her with two gold coins.

The sun had not yet rose so Jared walked his horse. He ate as he walked west from where he was. When the sun rose he climbed on his horse and rode in the direction given him. Jared understood the reason for the lady waking him so early was two. She did not wish anyone to see him leaving her home, and two; his journey was through some thick forest where he would not be able to ride his horse without risk to it. Jared rode on at a gallop, keeping a weary eye out for any signs of anything he thought not normal while he stuck to the course given him. It was several hours after the sun had rose that he shifted from straight west to north-west and headed up land.

The town homes became less and less and the sight of posted men here and there was evident. No-one approached him or cried out nor made any signal at his passing. But he knew they marked him well. He past the last pond in the town knowing it so as the ground went higher and higher. Soon he would have to unsit his horse and leave her behind. He could see the forest ahead but it was so thick he could not see through it. The trees seemed to be packed so tight, like a wall and he knew it would take some time to get through it on foot. It took him another twenty minutes before he had to dismount and leave his horse. He entered the forest cautiously looking for the signs the lady gave him. His rout continued northwest but the uphill trek began to level out some. His first marker was in sight and he would be heading straight west again.

Jared walked alone in the forest for a while before his ears were assaulted with the sounds of bow strings twanging. He drew his daggers and prepared to block the coming arrows. He turned and twisted slashing down arrow after arrow. The volley seemed as if it would never stop. The continuous sound of twanging bow strings rang loud in his ears. He tried running for cover behind trees but it was no good. The arrows struck him in the back as he blocked the ones coming straight at him. As he was hit he was jerked forward but stayed on his feet. The arrows continued to strike him but none penetrated because of his cape and mail shirt. But still the onslaught of arrows was annoying and becoming painful. The force of the arrows struck harder as the archers drew in circling him. He could see them clearly now and began to make his own assaults with his stars.

His foes eased their way toward him and continued letting loose arrow after arrow. He picked a direction and ran as fast as he could at his attackers. Several times he stumbled from the force of the arrows. Broken limbs lay about but he made sure not to trip over them. This time his adversaries seemed more prepared for him and they were determined. They were well positioned and supplied with plenty of arrows. Jared ran trying to keep some trees between him and the archers. He was moving fast and it was working for him. He fell two archers, one right in front of him and the other off to his right. He threw two more stars and hit one man in the eye and just missed the other man. He was closer now to some of the archers and their reloading of arrows was slower now. Jared ran head long at one man as he raised his bow and at the last moment he ducked behind a tree and threw a star at another man. Through all of this Jared noticed that none of the archers were posted in the trees, he won't complain about that.

A man dropped his bow and drew his sword charging Jared. He only made a few steps before he fell to one of Jared's stars. Jared quickly grabbed up the fallen man's bow and bundle of arrows. He let fly his own volley securing a spot for himself. As he let fly his own volley three men fell to him but he was nicked on the neck as he tried to dodge at the last moment. They drew in real close now and the arrows stopped as men drew swords. Jared smiled as he dropped the bow he had. Whatever chance they had of capturing him was just lost. They should have kept their distance. Jared drew his short sword and rushed into them with a feral growl. Two men quickly fell to his rage and Jared knew they were better archers than swordsmen.

Suddenly the wound on his neck began to burn and he knew he had to finish these men quickly. The arrow that struck him was poisoned. He parried the attack of one man and kicked out at another. He quickly changed direction as his hand shot out grabbing a man by the throat as he rushed him. His grip tightened and squeezed crushing the man's windpipe. Shoving him into another as he ducked an attack, a sword cut through the air above his head. Snatching stars from is belt and letting fly they caught his side opponents, one dead in the eye the other in the forehead. His sword cut the leg of another man as he jumped sideways cutting an attack short. Jared's hand shot up into the chin of one foe and as he flexed his wrist a blade shot out stabbing into the man's mouth. Jared withdrew it and swung at another cutting him deep on the cheek. Two swords came at him, he ducked one twisted into the other while dropping his sword he grabbed the man and turned him into the path of his own fellow. The cut deep into each other. Jared reach to retrieve his sword and had to draw his hand back. Blood squirted from the wound he just receive from it. He punched into the groin of a man standing over him and his left leg kicked out at another coming at him. He shattered the man's knee and rolled away grabbing up a fallen man's sword as he went to block a downward slash to his head.

Only three men remained and Jared hoped they too were bad swordsmen. His adrenaline was pumping and it allowed the poison to flow threw him. This was a typical poison and he had the antidote in one of his rings. He needed to take it soon or he would become faint and his muscles would lock up paralyzing him. He knew he didn't long. In the position he was in he stomped his heel hard enough to spring his boot-blade. He leaned to the side stretching out his leg. It darted out cutting one man in the stomach twice. Jared threw his sword like a spear at another man distracting him enough so he could finish off the man he just kicked in the stomach. The man that he punched in the groin was one of the two men left. Jared's arm began to twitch and his muscles tightened. He felt for his stars at his belt but only brought forth one. His right eye began to close and his mouth tightened as well. With his left hand he threw the star and shoved the same hand forward. His opponent blocked the star but didn't expect the blade that sprang from Jared's wrist stabbing him in the throat. One man remained and Jared could see the caution on his face as he held up his sword unsure to attack. Jared used this to his advantage. With his left hand he brought his right hand up and snatched the ring off his hand with is mouth. He twisted its cap while he watched his last foe circle him. The contents of the ring filled his mouth and he grimaced at its taste. His foe clearly began to see his condition and smiled at it. He clenched his teeth and raising his sword he rush at Jared. Jared allowed himself to fall to the side and in doing so he tripped the oncoming man. The man fell face forward and before he could right himself Jared used his last bit of strength, he sprang on him stabbing him in the back of his neck repeatedly with his wrist-blade.

Jared rolled on his back laying still trying to calm himself. He waited for the antidote to kick in and fight off the poison in his body. If he was attacked now there was nothing he could do to defend himself. He closed his eyes and just lay still.

16

Jared opened his eyes and jerked up to a scavenger bird landing on his chest. Shocked mad the bird bounced and flew away with a screech. After he got rid of the bird he tested his limbs. He flexed his hands and bent his arm sat the elbow, wriggled his toes in his boots and brought his knees up to his chest. Satisfied that he was functional he got up and retrieved his weapons. Since he was not being attacked he felt he had the time to do so. He found his short sword and daggers. Slowly he picked his stars from dead bodies and trees. He didn't like to leave any of his weapons behind. Many men lay dead and Jared walked past them and around them as if they were not really there. He looked around and righted himself in the way he needed to go.

There was a tree that had its limbs and branches that looked too pruned in a perfect circle. From there he traveled northwest again while looking for his next sign. The forest here was really thick and its roots lay above ground. Continuously stepping over roots, twisting, and ducking under limbs he still went in a northwest direction swatting away bugs and keeping clear of snakes and spiders that had no problem striking out at men. As he walked on he had wished he had brought a canteen. His mouth was dry and still had that nasty aftertaste of the potion he took. The poison used on that arrow was common and of three kinds. Two of which could be found in this very forest. The scinder spider and a plant called apuplicion. The other was from a frog from Chilang. A well-known combination used throughout the land. The poisons were meant to blind and paralyze you and mixed together they made you blackout.

Jared came upon his next sign as he walked on. This was something he had never seen. Being so close to the boarder he had not come this way before.

The soil itself seemed to change into a thick dark soil, rich soil. Berry bushes spouted wild here and there and the trees beyond and over them grew buds of blue flowers. He seen how it was possible for the lady he sought to dye all the parchments sky blue, and even the blanket as well. The berries and the flowers the trees produced would provide her with enough color to dye anything she wanted. He walked on until the berry bushes grew no more. Then he came upon a small river that separated the two kingdoms. From there he turned back straight west walking along the river banks opposite its flow. There really was no clear path to walk, with the river being the in the middle of the forest the vegetation was thick. Vines hung low, roots lay above ground and the thorn bushes slowed one to a careful pace. One he trekked until it all began to fade. He could tell that someone had cut he trees and pulled up the roots and bushes. The land was suddenly too clean and beautiful grass was grown and kept. Flowers grew in a line like a path. Off in the distance Jared spotted a house. He thought it weird because it was a well-built house and not some throw together shack. There was a yard with flower beds and a small barn in the back, and he could hear a dog barking. This place should not be here.

As Jared got closer the dog came running at him, it barked and snarled until he kicked it away. Jared came near to the front of the house and a young man stepped out from the side. A sword was strapped to his back and his face was not friendly at all. As Jared continued to the door the young man told him to stop.

"You do not belong here, turn around and leave." he said sternly.

Jared's gaze looked him over. He was tall, well-built and muscular. His eyes were serious and he stood as a ready fighter. He was not sure if this was the young man spoken of but he had no intentions of leaving. If the lady he sought was here, he would speak with her. "I have no wrong intentions here. I seek an older lady known as 'G', does she live here?" Jared asked.

By the young man's facial expression he knew the answer. But the young man instead told him the same thing. "You do not belong here. I advise you to turn around and leave."

Jared did not like this at all and stepped forward. "I am the Royal Messenger of King Charles of Jericho." the young man did not recognize his uniform and expressed no fear of him, obviously Jared thought he was ignorant. "Move from my path." Jared took a step forward but the young man blocked his way. Step for step he was matched and grew tired of this. He would not ask again. Jared drew his sword and just as fast the young man drew his. "Stand aside before I cut you down." Jared told him.

"Turn and leave, before I cut you down." the young man replied.

Jared struck forward like lightening. With the same speed and strength to match, the young man blocked Jared's attack. For just a split second Jared was puzzled. He needed to be sure of something so he struck out again. The young man, his stance was mirroring, from his sword work, his foot movement to his posture. This young man fought as would a royal messenger would. But this was impossible, there were no-more and he was too young. Jared knew that he was the last one to be trained as a royal messenger, and the young man had to be between his age and Caleb, more to Caleb's. But everything about this young man spoke the opposite of his thoughts.

The young man changed his stance from defense to attack. They each struck out and parried the other. No matter which way he went the other was there to meet and match. The young man was just as surprised too. Like Jared, he too acted as if no-one should be able to fight like him. Neither one of them was much for words now. Their swords clanged together fast and hard, sparks flew from metal meeting metal. Their feet kicked out at each other only to be blocked. Neither one could gain advantage. It was purely up to strength and endurance. Their swords locked and their bodies pressed together. Face to face they struggled to push past the others strength. Muscles strained and bulged, eyes locked and teeth clenched. They pushed off and again sparks flew from angry sword kisses. They ducked swings to the head and dodge hand strikes. Again Jared was surprised, as he shot forth his left hand and flexed his wrist; he sprang his wrist-blade but the young man tilted his head to the side just avoiding the blade. He should not have known of that Jared thought. Both men were furious now and fought with the intention of ending this now. They clashed and clashed again and again. Their strikes were so hard that jolts traveled up their arms. Swords fell and hands and feet flew at each other. They both knew the others style because it was the same. Their bodies clashed and they struggle to get the other into submission, but neither gained the upper hand. Jared was stronger but the young man was slightly faster. Again they pushed off each other, they sprang away, rolled and retrieved their swords. They jumped up, stood paused ready to attack, sword s raised, voices yelled and they jumped at each other again.

Both men were brought up short in their attack as a sword flew in stabbing the ground between them. A natural, unthinkable reaction from them both made them stop in their tracks, drop their swords and kneel. Not to each other but to the sword that separated them. Jared recognized the sword and his heart beat faster. There was only ever one like it to be made and weld. Years and years of training to the attacks and defense of that sword and its welder made Jared tremble. Could it be possible, could his master, trainer and friend Michael be alive? He was unsure and uncertain of the man in front of him that his eyes only moved up to glance at the young man and seen that he to knelt. Many thoughts raced through Jared's mind.

It had been years since he last seen that sword. Day in and day out he had to face it, attack it, block it, and respect it. The welder and trainer was his father. A man he loved and missed very much. Years ago he had left and never returned. Could he have come back? Could his father, Michael be here now?

Through years of discipline both men knew not to move or get up until told. They were both shocked to hear the voice of a lady instead of a man. The same they both expected and respected.

"Both of you stop this." she paused and coughed "Get up." her voice was weak but all command.

The young man rushed to her, "Mother, what are you doing?" he ran to her aid.

Jared stood to see the young man helping an older lady that leaned against a tree. She wore a sky blue dress. She was fragile with long gray hair. Jared approached cautiously, "My lady?" she leaned heavy upon her son but her eyes never left Jared. Her face expressed question, uncertainty. "The king has received your letters and bid me come fetch you. I am to make sure that you are brought back to him safely. I am the Royal Messenger, at your service." he said and bowed to her.

"A Royal Messenger?" she was skeptical. "Yes, yes you are. You are a Royal Messenger! Come here, let see you." she coughed then held her hand out to him. The young man stood and watched Jared cautiously. "Do you know who I am? Has the King Charles told you of me?" she asked Jared.

"No my Lady, he has not. He told me that you would tell me who I am instead. You would tell me all" he said.

"You are Jared." a tear ran down her cheek. She lay her hand on Jared's cheek. "You are Jared, my son; my first born son."

Both Jared and the young man looked at her in surprise. "I..." Jared shook his head, confused he did not know what to say. All his life he wanted to know, to find out who his mother was. To find out what happened to her, and now he was sent to her by the King. She sent for him. "I don't understand." he managed to get out.

"Help me inside and I will explain. I will tell you all, as King Charles said." The young man helped her stand straighter as she leaned on him. "Get those swords and bring them inside." she told Jared. He silently complied and followed them inside the house.

Jared leaned the sword against the wall when he entered the house. His own he placed back in its scabbard. He stayed at the door while the young man helped the lady, his mother to the couch. When she was seated she called for Jared.

"Jared, come here and sit by me; please." hesitantly he went. He waited for this moment for so long, but now it seemed unreal.

"Come." she said again patting the seat next to her. She told the young man to sit down as well. She coughed then cleared her throat. Taking a deep breath she looked from Jared to the young man, her son as well. She allowed a little chuckle. "So, you have met George, my son and your younger brother." she said to Jared then looked to both of them. "I will tell you who I am and who the both of you are." they looked at her confused. "I am Princess Georgette, elder and only sister of King Charles." this shocked them both. She held up her hand to stop any questions. "King Charles is my younger brother, we share the same father; King George. We do not share the same mother. My mother was Queen Silviah and I was their only child. For years the Queen, my mother; tried to bear another child for the king but could not. When she was a litter older she conceived but the child died at birth. So for many years I was King George's only child. He married again, to Queen Juliah and she bore Charles. The king's first and only son. But our father had much love for me and was tempted to change the traditions. He was going to name me his heir to the throne. A daughter as sole heir, he knew that I was capable. But, Queen Juliah being cousin to the Fontz conspired behind the king's back," she paused to cough then told George to get her some water to drink. When he returned she continued. "They said that I was a threat to Prince Charles and that he should be the one to rule, not me. Our father grew ill and they used this time to threaten me. They would not allow me to see the king and kept a watch on me. They thought to have me killed but exiled me instead. Charles was young and knew nothing of this. When the king, our father got well; they told him I ran off. Our father and Charles was heart struck for they both had much love for me. I was father's only daughter and Charles' only sibling. Our father lived on but was never the same. Before he passed on Charles was named heir then became king upon his passing.

As Charles' reign began his mother Queen Juliah had rallied the nobles and council to bring an end to the Royal Messengers, to let them go. But before this I sought the company of Prince Clifford of Starkens. We courted until he found out I was exiled from my own home. What he did not know was that I was with child, you Jared; my first born."

Jared had interrupted her story, "But we fought against them, twice."

"Yes I know, I know. I could never learn the reason, but you must realize that you came along long before the two kingdoms started warring. You, Jared are a prince; a prince of two kingdoms. I, Princess Georgette and now King

Clifford, are your parents." she allowed enough time for this to sink in then continued. "The older nobles and Queen Juliah had discovered that I still lived and had not left the kingdom that I still kept and gathered information from within the castle. They killed my informant and decided to have me killed as well. I could not be an exiled fugitive with a child to look after. So I sent you to the king and begged for his mercy. I sent him a letter begging that he take you in and care for you. Of course when they discovered what I had done they were furious, but could do nothing about it. This was around the same time that the nobles and council members succeeded in ending the service of the Royal Messengers. Charles had fought for them for a while.

When you were sent to him and he accepted cared for you, the queen said that you were a threat to his throne. You being the son of the first born, they wanted to kill you. They were never told who your father is. But Charles would have none of it and threatened to wipe out the whole family of anyone who even harmed a hair on your head. The price of your life, was silence. He was forced into silence, sworn to tell no-one, not even you that you were his nephew, a prince and son of a princess and neighboring prince. To protect you I see he decide to have you trained as a Royal Messenger. You were placed under Michael's care and training." she paused again to cough then drink some water. "I did not believe it, but it is true. Your training was amplified twice to that of a normal Royal Messenger to ensure your survival. In the middle of your training the council and nobles won the argument against the existence and training of children as Royal Messengers. They were all let go of the king's service. Your training was incomplete and to stop it, it would kill you. Charles refused that to happen. He kept Michael on to finish your training and when it was complete, he left the king's service as well. You are the last of the Royal Messengers. I see that it is all true" she paused in thought for a moment. "But out of fear the nobles had the messengers hunted, and upon finding them they were killed. Michael, however upon his leaving was on his way to seek refuge with the Starkens and had come this way when he found me. All I have told you, he has told to me. When he came upon me and seeing that I still lived, he vowed to protect me. We grew close and I bare him George" again she paused. She looked to George then back to Jared. "Yes, yes you two are brothers; my sons." she smiled and shook her head. "In battle is how you two greet each other. Boys will never change. She said still smiling. "Michael trained the two of you. He trained George just as he trained you, Jared. The difference between the two of you is that you are sworn to the service of the king and George is not. But both of you are my sons, raised and trained by Michael." She looked to George, "I know you are wondering what happen to your father, and why he left. He returned to his home, to be buried with his parents." she pointed to her room. "The trunk at the foot of my bed is where he kept his uniform and weapons. I put his sword there when he departed. All of it was to be given to you." George looked towards the room. Jared looked towards the sword resting against the wall were he left it. "I felt that you had no need of it yet. It would draw too much attention if people saw it." she was tired and her voice grew weaker as she talked. Just the retelling was taxing her but she felt that she needed to tell them, both of her sons needed to know the truth. She bid George to get her some more water and get some for Jared as well.

"Jared, I wrote many letters to Charles but could not leave any hint to where I live or how to respond. If he knew where I was he might have sent for me. It was not I, never was it I that threatened him; to his throne. It was his own mother and the nobles, then the Queen Alicene joined their plot. But I am old now Jared, and dying." George walked back in with the mugs. She drank, coughed clearing her throat. Jared drank his emptying it at once. "I wanted to see you before I died Jared. To lay eyes upon you, my first born son. I waited so long for this," as she spoke tears welled up in her eyes. "I could not keep you Jared. I could not risk my child's life every day. I, I just couldn't." her tears fell freely now and Jared swallowed hard fighting back his emotions. "Would you forgive me my son? Jared please, would you forgive me for sending you away?" she fell onto his arm and cried. "I am sorry my son, I am sorry." she repeated with her voice muffled in his shoulder. Jared held her tight and buried his face in her hair.

Jared had his answer now, he knew who his parents were. He knew why the king was so protective of him, even after he was grown. He knew why the king shed tears upon opening and reading the sky blue parchment. He knew why he demanded that this lady be brought back to him at all cost. He knew why he was sent and why people feared him more than the king himself. It was the revealing of who he was that scared them. The discovery of what they had done to his mother, the princess and sister of king Charles. This is why the nobles hated him so much and why they sought to kill him. Seeing him every day was a constant reminder of what they had done. Jared also knew now as he held his mother that the journey back to the castle would be more dangerous than anything he ever faced. They would stop at nothing to kill him. And as he held her tightly to himself, he knew that he would spare none that tried to stop him. He looked to his younger brother George, "We must return to the castle, the king wants her brought home. The princess, his daughter is to be engaged or he would have come himself. I am to bring her home safely to him at all cost, even at the cost of my own life if need be. You too are to come to the castle." He said to George. To the both of them he said, "We will need food. I was poisoned twice on the way here and one time it was with food." it did not come as a surprise that he was still alive. George and the princess knew of the Royal Messenger training. They were silent so he could continue. "I will trust no-one to feed you on the way. We will also need a carriage for you once we past the forest."

"I know another way without going through the forest. It will take another day's journey, but at least the road will be smoother." Princess Georgette said to Jared. Turning to George she said, "George, will see that we are provisioned enough for the travel."

"I will." he said.

"We are used to traveling back and forth into town and staying well prepared. Jared will you help him?" he answered by nodding his head yes. "We will leave as soon you two are done." she told them go and Jared followed George out of the house.

They went to the barn and Jared seen there was already smoked and salted meat hanging. He saw a small carriage and jugs for water. They set to fill the jugs and package the meat. They harnessed the two horses to the carriage. George had another one that he would ride. Jared had told him that he had left his horse behind and would retrieve it on the way. Within the half hour they were ready and brought the carriage to the front of the house. George knew that there would be bread and cheese packed by the time he got back. They both went in to help their mother. She was up and dressed, leaning on her cane.

"George, I, I lay out your father's uniform and weaponry. He would want you to have it." she faced Jared, "since Jared is the official Royal Messenger, if he does not object; I wish that you wear it on our journey. It will fit you." both George and their mother looked to Jared.

"I do not object, and would love to see someone else in a Royal Messenger uniform; besides just me."

George humbly nodded and went to the room to change. Jared carried the packages to the carriage and helped his mother in while they waited on George. The Princess decided to ride up front for the fresh air, telling Jared that when she tired she would go in the back. George came to the door dressed exactly like Jared and slid his father's sword in the scabbard strapped to his back.

Princess Georgette and her two sons, both raised by the Royal Messenger Michael, all headed back to the castle of King Charles.

17

Jared sat beside his mother on the carriage seat guiding the horses as his mother instructed him. George rode his horse beside them and the dog ran beside him. They rode west and southwest going around the forest Jared just traveled through. The ground was smooth for the carriage and the temperature was nice with a breeze every now and then. They rode in silence, not knowing what to say. It was uncertainty of acceptance from the other that they held back their words. George watched both of them from where he rode. He could see the tightness about them both. He watched Jared the most. He was slightly impressed with his uniform when he first arrived, now he too wore one just like it. George believed that he was the only one that could fight the way he was trained to. Now there was another with the same skills and abilities as himself. He thought that he was the only child and now finds out that he has an older brother. He has relatives he realized. An uncle and cousins and he would see them soon. His mother was a princess, royal blood, her brother the king had raised her oldest child and he sent for her to come home. What type of reception would they have? How would the king react to him, another nephew? He realized that he too was royal blood. George thought about many thing as he rode beside them. All the things he had missed because his mother was an exiled princess. Having done nothing wrong she was sent away because of what, jealousy. He did not know the queen or the nobles who had caused this on his on his mother, but he already had hard feelings against them by just hearing the story of what they did. He had even seen the hurt and anger in Jared's face as their mother told her story. He knew that Jared hoped to come across the nobles along the way back to the castle, he knew because he felt the same way.

Just after night fall Princess Georgette went inside the carriage and lay down. In no time she fell fast asleep to the rocking of the carriage. Jared continued on the path she told him and George rode in close to him.

"When do you think of stopping for the night, or don't you?" George asked.

"We will stop at mid-night, then set out again at dawn to give you and the horses rest. Will that be enough?" Jared asked in return.

"Yes that will be fine." George was silent for a moment then asked. "I take it that you are very used to traveling so, or either you have a potion to keep you up for long periods."

"Have you not been taught the travelers rest?"

"No." George said shaking his head. "What might that be?"

"It is a sleep that last only a few hours but allows you to stay woke for at least two days. Two days of hard travel. It was part of our training since we were sent on many missions, some far and some close. But because of the danger to us and our mission, we had to be able to stay woke and alert as long as possible."

"Perhaps my father thought that I would not need it. My, our mother had no reason or intention of traveling anywhere far."

They rode in silence for some time then Jared asked, "What was it like growing up with her?"

"Lonely." George answered.

"I figured that. It was no different in the castle. I was shunned most of my life. I mean I had Michael who trained me and the king's protection but, I, I guess because of who I was and then what I became; even surrounded in the castle I was still alone. People were scared to talk to me. They didn't even want to look at me. Rooms went silent when I entered them. When Michael left, I was truly lonely. The king, he was busy being a king and for a while the princesses weren't born yet. But when they came along, their mother Queen Alicene, tried to keep them away from me. She tried to anyway. Princess Elizabeth is headstrong and stubborn. She made it her business to seek me out. Her and her friend Caleb. I taught them both many things. To both of them I taught politics and history, but with Caleb I taught him how to fight as well. He has not the same complete training as we do, the magic resistance and potions, and strength. But he is naturally strong and his style of fighting is like ours. He is a good young man, a little younger than yourself. He has been engaged to the princess, or will be anyway."

"Did you not leave before this contest started?"

"Yes I did."

"Then how do you know that this Caleb will engage the princess?"

"I know Caleb. He is the best of those chosen suitors. Unless someone cheats, he will win."

They spoke as they rode on. Both having many questions to ask the other about how they lived. Jared had watched for signs of mid-night and when it came, they stopped. He looked in on the princess and seen that she slept still. He left the carriage and went over to where George sat propped up against a tree. He tried instructing him on how to put himself in the travelers rest, and encouraged him to try. He told George that if he was able to accomplish it or not, he would make sure he was woke before dawn.

As George lay down and tried to sleep, Jared walked about. He tried to keep control of his thoughts and emotions as he walked on. The night was a normal one, busy with the noise of night creatures. He had not been this way before in his travels to the Starkens and was not sure if the other nobles would guess that they would travel this road back. They had obviously knew he was coming to see the princess, but had they known that he would bring her back. Had they expect an older lady to travel through the forest? Perhaps they had not known of this way. He seen that it was clear of any signs as he walked. Jared may not have known this part of land, but he knew that people weren't trained as good scouts anymore. If someone had come this way he would have picked on their trail by now. Nothing was amiss so he headed back to the others. There was no rush, George was a capable fighter and they had that noisy dog with them.

He did not know what to do with himself. He waited a long time for this and now, what was to be done about it. He smiled to himself thinking of the past rumors of the king being his father, ha. If they only knew that King Charles was his uncle; his mother's younger brother. He now had his reason for why the king was so over protective of him as he grew. Why he was able to stay in his chambers. Why he was the only person who could approach the king at any time fully armed. The mysterious royal messenger was family to him, and his daughters. He knew that the princess would be ecstatic to find out that he was her older cousin. She would try to use that against people. That made him laugh.

Jared made it back to his mother and brother and leaned against a tree. A crazy thought struck him and that was not good. What would the nobles and citizens, the council do when they found out that the king had a close male relative, a nephew. They could force him into proclaiming him the heir, being that he was older than George. It was a right of relation and tradition. The king having no male sons of his own would have to choose from the males closest in relation to him. The males outstripped the females, even of the Kings own lions when it came to succession to the throne. This is what King George thought to disrupt. Now he really realized why Queen Alicene didn't want this, his history and relation discovered. Jared could demand the king follow tradition and the knowledge to bind the king to do it. He would, could be the next king of Jericho. He shook those thoughts away. No, no, he didn't want that at all. What he actually wanted was to be free of any obligations, free to come and go as he pleased. Free to have a normal life.

Lost in his thoughts the dawn came upon him. It was the Princess that drew his attention. She had climbed to the outside of the carriage and was trying to get down. He got up and went to assist her.

"Thank you, Jared." she told him. She needed to relieve her bladder and called the dog to her as she went into the bushes. George woke up with his hand on his sword when he heard the dog barking. They did not speak much on the princess' return. They broke their fast and started on their travel again.

On the way Jared searched for his horse in his mind. He learned to do this from the Bestles horse breeders. It was almost like going into a travelers rest or easing your energy essence to flow in a fight. You simply channel the energy elsewhere. He channeled it into his horse instead of within himself. He had only ever done it once before in his travels.

As they ended their travel around the forest they now headed east opposite the way he came. Jared tried to guide his horse by relaying images of what he saw. It was about an hour till he met up with his horse. He did not mount her but continued to drive the carriage.

"We will make one stop, to a friend of yours. The one who guided me to you. Do you trust her? Jared asked the Princess.

"Yes, she and her son are trust worthy."

"Then we will bring them with us. The boy will drive the carriage, and his mother will attend to you." no-one disagreed with him. His last words were really statements of fact and not questions. They made their way back to the inner town and Jared's horse followed. Many eyes were cut their way and people ran to get out of their way. Fear on them was evident. Jared had come this way alone and now there was another just like him on his return. What cold this mean? The princess went back inside the carriage so that the people could not see her.

Jared led the carriage to the home of the lady who assisted him. This time it was still evening but even so Jared did not mind being seen going up to her home. He had no intention of leaving her behind, so it would not matter who saw them or not.

All three of them dismounted. George, Jared, and their mother; Princess Georgette went to the door. Jared knocked loudly, the door opened to a crack as the lady peeked out. She seen the princess, a lady she knew as G and when she seen George and Jared, both dressed alike; her face showed caution.

"It is alright, Martha. These are my sons." bringing a surprised expression to Martha's face.

"Oh my, I did not know." Martha said.

"No-one really knew, may we come in?"

"Yes, yes. Oh I'm so sorry. Yes come in." she said opening the door for them. Her son stood behind her.

It was Jared who spoke first when they entered the home. "We do not have much time. From what I understand, you have been a good friend to the princess." he said without thinking much into it. But he realized right away that Martha had not known.

Martha's eyes widened and her mouth fell open. "Princess?" she breathed then fell to her knees.

"No, no please. Martha, get up." the princess told her. "Get up Martha, we are friends."

"Princess I, I did not know, I..."

"Again, many people did not know." she shook her head looking at Jared. "I have not been called by that title in so many years. Please forgive my son, he did not know and spoke eagerly." she then let Jared speak again.

"We are returning to the king and need someone to tend to," he paused looking at the princess, "my mother. You can see to that while your son sits the coach. Me and...my brother George will ride beside the carriage." he said without question, but the princess interjected.

If you do not mind coming along. I would be grateful for your company."

"Oh yes, yes. I will come with you. How could I say no?" Martha said.

"If you do not wish to, you don't have to come along, Martha." the Princess assured her.

"I want to. You have been a good friend to me. I will help you G, um I mean Princess."

"Please continue to call me G."

"We must hurry and be on our way." Jared spoke up. "Gather up only what you will need for the journey. Everything else will be supplied for you when we reach the castle.

Martha quickly picked out a dress and some papers from her room. She sent her son to gather up some food supplies and let the donkey loose. They would not have need of it and she did not want the animal trapped in the barn. Martha and her son left their little home and joined the Princess in her carriage. Her son Jacob grabbed the reigns and followed after Jared and his brother. They were headed to the castle now. Jared guided them until mid-night giving them all a chance to rest. So far the journey was uneventful. "Do you think you can accomplish the travelers rest yet?" he asked George as they posted up by the carriage.

"I did not last night, but I will try again." George said.

"Try to do so. It has been a while since I got any real rest. I am tired and will rest tonight." he told George. "I will wake you in three hours time and we will switch guard then."

"You plan to set out at dawn?"

"Yes."

"That will barely give you, what… two hours rest?"

"It will be enough. Now try to get some sleep. The travelers rest, try it. I will wake you soon." he did not wait for an answer, he walked away intending to scout ahead. In doing so, again he felt nothing amiss.

When it came time to wake, George was unsure if accomplished the rest or not, but told Jared he was rested enough. Jared traded places with George and in no time he was fast asleep.

Jared did not need anyone to wake him. When the dawn came he automatically woke well refreshed with it. George was up and he seen Jared stir and sit up. He went and woke Jacob. They broke their fast and set out.

Both George and Jared were alert as they rode on. Jared had thought it strange that they, or he was not attacked as of yet. He had asked Martha if she had seen anything strange happening in the time since he left her. She replied she had not and her son agreed with her. Still Jared was not satisfied and rode on cautiously. He had to stay at the pace with the rest of them being that their horse were not as strong as his and the carriage could only go so fast. They kept a steady pace and by evening Jared had sent George ahead to scout for them. From time to time the princess came to sit out of the cover of the carriage.

George had gone out twice and now when it was night he came rushing back to the group. "Just past the end of town there are men gathered about. When they saw me they let arrows fly at me. I guess they thought that I was you."

"Did they give chase?" Jared asked.

"They come shortly behind me."

"Then let us go meet them."

18

"Princess" Jared called, "Please go back inside and stay. George tells of a band coming our way. We are going to meet them." the princess climbed in with Martha. "Keep them at a steady pace." he told Jacob, "only if you see that you will be accosted then go at all speed. Do you understand?"

"Yes." Jacob answered.

Jared could tell that the bot was nervous but hoped that he could hold it together. Jared and George tightened the grip on their horses reign and raced off. Determination was on both of their faces.

It was twenty minutes until they rode upon the band of soldiers. They were spotted and the soldiers charged them both with drawn swords and yells. Jared and George drew their long swords and dismounted at a charging run. Both men dressed in black, swords drawn and capes billowing behind them as their long black braid bounced from side to side and their metal caught the glint of light. Their swords hummed through the air and the sound of metal striking metal rang out.

The force of Jared's swing sent a jolt of pain up the arm of his foe. The man almost dropped his sword and tried to recover but Jared was fast in turning his sword in a downward slash cutting the man deep in his lower side. Jared didn't stay to see the man fall, his next foe was at him.

George swung high at a charging man forcing him to draw up short. This gave him time to turn with a jumping knee into the flank of a man at the side of him. This man was about to swing his sword at Jared's head. But just as quick George brought his sword into a backward slash cutting into the arm of another man. A sword came in high to strike him and he parried its attack.

His sword flew fast blocking the attack of two men. One of them lost his head as Jared swung his sword mightily cutting through his neck.

Their enemies gave them no time to dwell on any fallen for as they came at them. George side stepped an attack and turning from it stepped into another. He brought his sword up to block it and kicked out backwards into the knee of a man who just missed him, his sword clashing with the man in front of him. George jerked his head to the left causing his braid ball to fly out. The man to his right caught the metal ball to his cheek smashing his cheek bone. He ducked a swing and coming in low cut into the leg of the man in front of him. He heard the voice of Jared telling him to stay down.

Jared's sword swung over George's head blocking a downward slash of the sword coming at him. Jared stepped around George as he scrambled away staying low. He stomped his boot heel, its blade sprang out to catch a man in the thigh. He turned from bringing up his sword to block an attack coming down at him. Both Jared and George were in their element of fighting. All the training that Michael gave them stayed clear in their mind. Their eyes stayed alert as they watched their enemies every maneuver. They also watched out for each other and tried to compliment the other's movements. They fought along-side each other while keeping themselves from being overwhelmed. Ducking from and switching foes, man and after man fell to their blades. When it was over, whoever was not dead they walked around and finished them off without any mercy.

Jared called for his horse and with it came George's. They mounted and raced off to catch up with the carriage that passed them as they fought.

Jacob was frightened and his hands trembled as he held on to the reigns. He could hear horses coming up from behind him as he was tempted to whip the horses into a charging run. But he thought of Jared and George, as he passed them many men lay dead on the ground. And no-one was atop a horse. He assumed their fight was coming to an end. It was a relief to him when he heard Jared's voice calling out to him. Jacob relaxed a little bit but kept the horses at the same pace. He turned about and seen both Jared and George on either side of him and he managed a short tight smile for them both.

"Has anyone approached you?" Jared asked.

"No, not from the front of the carriage." Jacob answered

Martha stuck her head out of the carriage, "Is the Princess alright?" Jared asked when he saw her.

"Yes," she replied. "She asked if the two of you were okay."

"Tell her all is well. We will continue on at this pace for a while. Let us know if either of you need to stop."

"We will," Martha said and ducked back inside.

Their little party rode on a while with George and Jared fully alert, watching for any signs of trouble. Well into the night they passed homes and taverns and people who darted out of their way. There was a group of armed men running about and they thought they were about to attack, but the men paid them no re their carriage no mind. They rode unhindered until the midnight. Jared had told Jacob to stop the carriage which he complied happily. When Jacob stepped down from the carriage he rub his leg and backside. He then stretched and walked about. The horses were fed and loosed to roam about while Jared horse stayed closed to them. They had all eaten and drank and as soon as they were done Jacob stretched out and was fast asleep. Martha and the princesses wanted to stretched their legs so George went ahead of them checking the area, he came back to tell them it was okay and they went to handle their lady business. When they returned the princesses called to Jared.

"Come here Jared. I am well rested and want to walk some will you come talk to me?"

"What is it you wish to talk about Princesses?" He asked

"Jared pleased, I'm your mother, call me so."

He did not reply right away but thought of how he should reply. "I have never used that word in that way my whole life. It is strange to me for I never addressed anyone so,"

"There is no one in the whole castle you have thought as a mother?"

"No, not one. It was Michael who raised me, Than the king who guarded me." He fell silent. The princesses watched him as he walked. "Everyone shunned me," He picked up from his thoughts "Until the Princesses Elizabeth got old enough to walk about the castle on her own."

"Jared I, I am sorry u had to live so, so isolated. I did not mean for your life to be like that."

"No, Mother, You did what you thought best. And we are both alive because of it."

"Has Charles never spoke of me, not once? Not even on accident?"

"I am sorry, but no. No one never has to my knowledge. The first I learn of you was the night I was sent for you. And still I did not know who you were to me, or the king." Jared had looked down on her small form as they walked. He could tell it hurt her to hear this. But why could he do to comfort her. He had to tell her the truth. They continued to walk and talk. The princess asked many questions about the young princess and what nobles were still around. Who were the current servants in the castle, who lead Charles' army, where and when had King George been laid to rest. All the questions she had asked Michael and more. They had headed back to the carriage and talk some more.

Jared told her of all he knew and could remember. He had questions of his own. Had the prince of Starkens ever found out that he had a son, how come she could not be accepted by them, had Lord Kenneth known that she lived on his lands all these years, how come no one never came at her once she had George, he answers were simple cut and dry. She told it as she knew it to be. Before the dawn came the princesses had went inside the carriage. Martha had asked if they should get an early start, but Jared told them they could still wait to the dawn. The horses needed their rest more than the humans, and so did young Jacob.

When the dawn came they harness the horses roused Jacob, and they broke fast they said out at once. Jared and George took turn ridding ahead every now and then. They both came back with same report. They had spotted armed men watching about that paid them no attention Jared dint like the looks or sound of it. Something brewing and he needed to find out what was going on.

It was mid-morning before they came upon another troop of men as they entered the town of Glassboro. Jared could no longer wait so he stopped them.

"You sir, what is this gathering of men about?"

"Civil war! The old nobles are going to war with the king!" he shouted

"When has this been declared?"

"Three days hence to my knowledge. It is also rumored that the king has declared war on the kingdom of Chamelle. Against King Perciville.

"Is that to be true?"

"From what I have been hearing it is. All able bodied men are ordered to report to their lords."

Jared road off to catch up with his party. He told them of what he heard. He and George were on alert now. Jared had told the princess and Martha they had to stay inside from now on. At least until they had to stop. For the rest of the morning and into the noon they continued to see group of men gathering. Black smiths hard at work and women folk clothing their children closely. War was a busy and uncertain time among the common folk. It wasn't until late that evening that they were attacked by Lord Robert's men. A group of sixteen men came at them and fell to them before they continued on. They were not bothered again for the next of the night or the next day. They needed to make up time for Jared was anxious to get back to the castle. He had Jacob and his mother, Martha take turns at the reigns, while one rest and slept the other ruled on. When they came into Lakewood they had to get extra padding for the carriage. A few times along the way arrows flew at them from hidden spots. Most of them were aimed at the carriage and not Jared or George.

They had stop to cover the carriage and switch horses for fresher ones. Jared had to use the authority of his post and the king's ring to get the horses. People were preparing for war or to either leave the area, no one wanted to part with their good horses. Both Jared and George had used this time to get some rest for themselves. They were two days travel away from the castle and Jared wanted to make the rest of the journey without stopping. It was dawn when they woke, broke fast and set out. Jacob was the rings and the princess and Martha were tucked inside the carriage with its extra leather draped over it.

Jared and George continued there vigilant watch at the carriage side. Their way was cleared and silent the whole morning they had seen no guards or mounted men about. It was a drastic changed and Jared did not like it at all. No one was outside their homes, but many times he seen heads and faces peeping out windows. George had road ahead almost an hour and when he returned he told of the same thing. Jared had thought to ride ahead himself but something nagged him, turned his stomach into knots and kept him at the side of the carriage.

They road on into late noon when Jared horse began to toss her head wildly and their dog barked and growled at nothing. The sound of thunder rolling could be heard ahead of them than the ground began to tremble. Jared could clearly hear it was the sound of men and horses. George's mouth dropped and his eyes widen just as Jacob did. Hundreds of men raced at them and Jared knew them to be Lord Robert's men, men not on the king's side he shouted to George.

"How good are you with your daggers?"

"Michael, my father taught me well." George answered. Shaking off the shock.

"Good than, this will be a close fight. Long swords will be an inconvenience and short swords will get in the way as well. We need to get in every hit we can with both hands, and make it all count well. The daggers will allow us to do that." Jared's face was serious and George took courage from him seeing how he was ready to handle this as if it were just another part of his everyday life. He set his mind to looking past the number "George", Jared called to him, "our mother must go to the castle. You and I are her only hope. Can you handle this?

George took a deep breath and answer "I believe this is what I was born and trained for. Jared, I am with you in this all the way."

Jared turned to Jacob. "Young man, do not stop this carriage for nothing. Do not stop until you see the King's castle. Do you understand me?"

"Yes sir. I, I do."

"Race on then. Go now."

George and Jared raced ahead at full speed. Their minds set on what must be done. Their training coming to the forefront of their thought. As they raced they assessed the situation. As Jacob snapped the reigns of the horses the carriage picked up speed and was right behind the two men. The last two trained in the way of a royal messenger. Train by the same man. Friend to one, father to the other. They rode into a mass of shouting armed men.

19

Jared drew his short sword and speared it at the first man in sight. With their faces set their hands went flew action. Both men fought knowing that they could not lose this battle. Their mother's life depended on it. They used their daggers and wrist blades to strike and block. They twisted and turned, kicked and side stepped from attack after attack. Many times they used the mass of men against themselves, they turned aside their enemies' blades to fall into their own fallen men.

Jacob rode on as the two men fought this army. He knocked down a group of men that tried to stand in his way of the carriage as he whipped the horses on. Two men on horses raced behind the carriage thinking to take it from behind. To their surprise a hand came from the curtain holding a cross bow and let fly an arrow into the face of one man and he fell from his horse. As quickly as it withdrew it appeared again and fell the other man before he decided to reign in his horse. But Jacob knew nothing of this as he raced on snapping the reigns of the horse.

Jared was very good at sliding his dagger into their joints of his opponents. At the underarm, side flank, bottom belly, neck, groin, and behind the knee. As he blocked and lifted the sword of his opponents with one hand, he would strike out with the other scoring hit after hit, disabling a man from the fight. When Jared fought it was never as if in vulnerable. He fought as if he was on the last limb and it was mandatory to score a killing blow to save his own life. Every hit counted and slowed his enemies down. Many time it was the material of his uniform and mail shirt that saved his life over and over. There were just too many men for moving room and him not to get hit. He and George got separated at the onset of this fight and could not worry about the other.

But he chanced a glance his way and seen that he was very sufficient with his daggers and braid ball.

Every movement that Jared made was a strike to his opponents. His wrist muscles burned tight as he continuously used his wrist to block strikes at him and flexed to withdraw its blade to cut the faces, throats and other parts of his foe. Over and over he stamped his boot heel springing its blade kicking into the calves and groin area of men he fought. Man after man leaped away trying to get clear but Jared use them as shields and pushed them into their fallen men.

Jared was pressed hard by three men until he was forced backward and tripped over a fallen man. The men sprang at him. The first was stopped by a boot blade. Jared rolled over and as he got up knocked into another man who swung backward wildly without looking and cut his own fellow deep in the neck. Jared stabbed the man in the back twice before he could turn around. The third man had to push his fellow out of the way to keep from being forced backward and slowing his attack. But Jared used this to his advantage. He sprang forward cutting one man in the neck, stabbing another under his arm and slashing the face of another before his foe could step up to him. He brought up his daggers blocking the man's falling word and snatched up his knee into the man's groin. To keep some men at bay he pushed this man into another then quickly threw out both arms turning about in a circle with his daggers. They took a step back and Jared stepped in striking blows to disable them.

George's braid ball smashed into the mouth of one man knocking out his teeth and filling his mouth with blood. His hands moved like lightening, as if he held nothing in them. He dare not stand still from getting surrounded. Men cautiously came at him and he jumped about over fallen men and cutting down others. His head jerked this way and that smashing his braid ball into the faces of his foes. He yelled and charged men not giving them a chance to decide to stand against him or not. His black uniform was stained darker with the spilled blood of his opponents. He looked wild and berserk as he slashed and cut down man after man. His foes were weary of him than the other black clad figure but could fare no better with that one either, if they could get out of the path of this one.

George leaped into the air yelling at his foe, his knee leading the way. Before he landed he struck out at one man to his right with a backward cut. He was barely on the ground before he was in the air again turning with a side kick to a man whose stomach fell open to his boot blade. When he landed he had to sidestep a man who came at him. Two fast strikes fell the man in front of him and a hard swinging elbow to the face of another slowed him down. George threw his dagger into the eye of one guy an d with that free hand snatched several stars from his waist and threw them scoring with each. One guy he hit in the back of the neck as he raised his sword to strike Jared from behind. With one dagger and his wrist blade George made his way roughly to retrieve his other dagger, snatching it from the socket of the dead man. As he bent to pull it free he was knocked from behind and fell into two men. He knocked them both down and stabbed down on them quickly before they could recover. The man that knocked him down leaped over his fellow man and was about to bring his blade down on him but caught a dagger in his mouth as he yelled, the man's head jerked back and his attack ruined.

Jared passed George on his way to retrieve his dagger. The men locked eyes briefly and saw the spilled blood of their enemies about them. There was no time to speak as George had to block a sword coming at him. He turned slashing a man's midsection and seen at the same time five men literally jump on Jared bringing him down. He yelled his furry but could not get to him. His path was blocked by enemies. Neither of them caught a break in the fight being overwhelmed by the number of their enemy. However, they continued to fight on. George thought it was evident that they would die this day fighting so that their mother could return to the home of her childhood, the king's castle.

While the carriage was on the way to the castle, three more men fell to cross bow bolts unknown to Jacob. He kept his face steady and his hands tight on the reigns. He had to keep the carriage moving. He rode on and on hoping to see the king's castle soon. His heart dropped at the sound of thundering hooves and charging men. They came on at him and he snapped the reigns yelling at the horses to go faster. His nerves were on edge but he knew that he could not stop, would not stop the carriage. They yelled out for him to stop and he yelled for the horses to go faster. His mother chanced a peep out of the carriage curtain and gasped at the sight of the charging men. The Princess was next to stick her head out. Upon seeing the men she yelled for Jacob to stop.

"They are the king's men Jacob. You must stop!" she placed a hand on Jacob's shoulder.

He turned to face her, "But… Jared, he…he told me not to stop. He said no matter what … don't stop…he told…"

"It's okay Jacob, but he did not know that the king's men were coming. You must stop for them." she leaned forward and took hold of Jacob's hands. He eased up on the reigns and the horse slowed then finally came to a stop.

The king's men circled the carriage. A man rode his horse to the side of the carriage, "who are you and where are you headed?" he asked.

"We seek the king, we are coming at his orders."

"Who are you?" the man asked the older lady, "who else is with you?"

The lady sighed then gathered her courage and spoke loudly, "I am Princess Georgette, elder and only sister of King Charles."

All of the mounted men dismounted and knelt to her. The young man who spoke first was the first to rise when she told them to. "Your Highness, I am Caleb; son of Lord John. We have heard that the Royal Messenger was to bring you home and we also heard that he was near. I, I don't see him about. Please tell me that my friend is alright."

"He is accosted by many men, Lord Roberts's men. He and George are a ways back fighting them."

"How do they fare?" Caleb asked with concern.

"I know not. Well over a hundred men fight them."

"My pardon, Your Highness," Caleb said as he mounted his horse. "But I must aid him. Some of these men will see you to the castle. It is a pleasure to finally meet you." Caleb barked some orders and twenty men stayed with the princess to escort her carriage to the castle. Caleb and the rest of the men raced off to assist Jared and this George fellow.

Jared swung wildly with his long sword keeping men at bay. With his right eye closed and a deep gash to the side of his leg he struggled to stay standing. George at his back held his left arm that hung lose at his side. The advantage of many men turned against them. Their foe was unsure now that so many men lay dead at their feet. Their enemies had used their own dead fellows to trip them up by forcing them one way.

Once Jared was down after trying to retrieve his dagger, it took him a great while to get back to his feet. He rolled about the ground kicking and slashing out but everywhere he turn an enemy was there to meet him. Only the fact that he still had his stars saved him as he threw them up at his enemies giving himself a chance to roll over and to his feet. He was sorely bruised from the stomps and kicks he received while on the ground. The gash to his side, he got trying to roll away. The one to his leg, was the first he receive upon falling. Several times he was kicked to the head, but eventually he drew his long sword and cut at their feet as they came near.

George did not fare well either being hit in the back of the head twice with the hilt of a sword. One of the men managed to grab hold of his braid and bring him down. He was immediately attacked. It was his wild and berserk way of fighting that kept them from afflicting too much harm on him. Over a hundred men fell to them but they could not finish this fight. From the time they had fallen, they received wound after wound and were now in very bad shape. It was now that their enemies used every advantage against them. They were now being circled by the last seventeen men. George could hear horses coming their way fast but he held on to whatever courage he had and with Jared, tried to hold their ground. He told Jared that it was a pleasure to have met him and fight at his side, but Jared told him that they were not dead yet.

118

With the last of their strength, both of them stepped forward swinging their long swords. Both men were attacked at once but it didn't not last long. When they fell to the ground exhausted no more attacks came.

Jared could hear shouts and the thwang of arrows as they struck. He expected to feel them cut deep into his flesh but none penetrated. He was fading out into blackness when he heard his name being called. Before his eyes shut he thought he seen the face of his friend Caleb close by him, then all went black.

The enemies they fought long and hard all lay dead about them. George lay still as some other men came to their aid. He had never in his life fought like this before and didn't know if he would ever in his life do so again. A young man not far from his age stood over him.

"Are you George?" he asked. "My name is Caleb, I am a friend of the Royal Messenger. Can you sit up?"

George managed to lift his head and men came to help him up. Caleb shook his head looking at George, "I did not know there were any more Royal Messengers. You are in bad shape."

"I am no Royal Messenger. This uniform belonged to my father."

"Oh, the princess had not told me."

"You saw my mother?"

This puzzled Caleb, "You mean the lady with the princess?"

"No Caleb. The princess is my mother, and Jared's as well."

Surprised shown on Caleb's face and he looked around to see if anyone else caught.

"I tell you no lie. Has she made it to the castle?

"She is on the way. We set out when we heard that Jared was near. I came across her and was told of you, we came right away. We need to get the two of you up so we can leave."

"Can you retrieve my weapons first?" George asked.

"I will have the men do so." Caleb told the men what to look for. He helped George up and on a horse. Jared was laid over another. The weapons were retrieved and Caleb and his men carried George and Jared to the castle. They had to travel at an easy pace so as not to jerk Jared about too much. Caleb had met the princess and now had a chance to rescue his friend Jared. He found out that the princess was Jared's mother, and that he had a younger brother, not much older than himself. The day had turned out to be a good one so far.

That is until he seen the princess' carriage laying on its side. He rushed forward to find all of his men dead along with men from Lord Robert's men. The lady that accompanied the princess lay dead with a sword in her stomach. There was no sign of the boy, Jacob nor the princess. "Search the area!" Caleb yelled to his men. "See where they may have been taken." he then dismounted and walked over to the carriage. When he ducked and looked inside, he breathed a sigh of relief. The boy Jacob held a bloody sword in his shaking hands. The princess lay propped against the side of the carriage with a bow in her hands.

"Your Highness, are you alright?" he asked her.

"We will be fine. We were set upon shortly after you left us."

"All the men are dead, on both sides. The Royal Messenger, Jared and George are with us. Your sons still live, but we need to get them help. Both of them are in bad shape." Caleb called his men back. They righted the carriage, fetched and harnessed the horse then placed Jared inside with the princess. George sat beside Jacob in the coach bench. Caleb and his men escorted them back to the king's castle, where men awaited them at the drawbridge.

20

Trumpets could be heard blowing loudly and repeatedly, Princess Elizabeth ran down the hall past people until she reached the balcony overlooking the drawbridge. She seen that her father was already there.

"Is it Caleb? Has he returned? Father I don't see anyone"

"Calm yourself, they will be here." King Charles told her.

Soon after King Gaston and Prince Conrad came along with Princess Bethal. They all stood upon the balcony and waited to see who was approaching. Guards stood at the ready down on the ground. A group of the king's men returned and with them a carriage. Princess Elizabeth was relieved and could not contain it upon seeing Caleb. She wanted to call to him, but something was wrong. Where were all the men that left with him? Several men guided riderless horses and Jared did not seem himself.

"Who is that?" Princess Bethal asked.

"I thought there was only one Royal Messenger left. Who is that?" King Gaston seconded.

"I, I do not know. But Jared is truly the last of the Royal Messengers. It looks like it might be him, but...it is not him." King Charles said and walked away from the balcony. Everyone followed him as he made his way down to the ground level. They all wanted to know who this man was, what happened to the rest of their men, and where was the Princess Georgette.

Caleb rode his horse to the front of the line and announced himself and the return of the Princess Georgette, even though he had already sent a man ahead of their approach. The men hurriedly made way and the party rode on in. Caleb sent servants to fetch medics right away. He dismounted and handed the reigns to a stable boy. Caleb helped George down from the coach when he almost fell. The back of the carriage was cut open and the princess was aided out. She stood leaning on her cane as she watched several men help carry Jared out of the carriage.

The Princess Elizabeth ran ahead of everyone and slowed when she seen two men dressed in the Royal Messenger uniform. Shock spread across her face when she realized it was Jared that lay on the ground. She did not know the other man that stood propped up by the soldiers.

King Charles approach slowly. Disbelief shown on his face. First he saw another Royal Messenger badly wounded. Then he saw another laid out on the ground unconscious, then he spotted the lady with the long gray hair, leaning on a cane. Her dress was dingy and ruffled, but it was definitely the color of sky blue. Caleb stood beside, her looking down on the unconscious Royal Messenger the soldiers just eased to the ground. The soldiers noticed the king and made way for him. Caleb went to him immediately to explain. King Charles could not take his eyes off the small form of the lady.

"Yes Charles, it is me. You have sent for me and I have come." Princess Georgette told him.

King Charles tore his eyes away and looked down on the Royal Messenger. "He still breaths, but just barely. He fought well, many men Charles. You, you kept my son. Thank you, Charles."

Still the king had not said a word. He was overwhelmed with emotion. Slowly he knelt down beside Jared. "I sent him out alone. I am responsible. I, I did this to him." he picked up Jared's limped hand and held it. "The medic," he said softly. "Where is the medics?!" his voice rose. He turned his head this way and that then yelled for the medics. King Charles stood picking up Jared up in his arms. Barely able to stand he stumbled forward. "Medics!" he yelled. "My nephew, my nephew is hurt! Medics!" he stumbled on with Jared in his arms. For the first time he was able to let go of his emotions. He was able to let everyone know that the Royal Messenger that he kept close to him all these years was his nephew, his family.

A team of medics rushed forward, some took Jared from the king's hands while others assisted George and checked on the Princess Georgette. King Charles called for Caleb and asked him to explain again what happened. Caleb told him how they came upon the carriage, seen Jacob riding like a daemon was after him, spoke with the Princes and her telling them that Jared and George fought a ways behind them. He told how they came upon the fight and seen both men fall. His men finished off the rest Lord Robert's men, then on their return they found the Princess' carriage had been attacked. All were dead except the boy and the princess. King Charles had already noticed the boy and seen that he was still in shock and uncertain of his surroundings. He decided that he would question him later.

As they made their way to the medics quarters the king turned to the group and apologized. "I apologize, my emotions got the better of me. King Gaston, Prince Conrad, and Princess Bethal; please allow me to introduce you to my elder and only sister, Princess Georgette and my nephew George."

They were walking quickly and the greetings were rushed. King Gaston told King Charles that he would excuse himself and his children from their group. To allow them time to speak with one another. "This is a time for reunion and pain for you my friend. It need not be mixed with politics or non-relatives. I will catch up with you when things have settled some." King Charles had clasped King Gaston's hand and thanked him. King Gaston had told his children to follow him and allow the king some time for privacy.

King Charles sent Princess Elizabeth with them, he told her that she could see them later when they were cleaned up and feeling better. He went on ahead with the medics and his nephews. Caleb fell back and went with Princess Elizabeth.

Later on that evening while the medics were working with Jared and George, King Charles walked with Princess Georgette. Together they went to her old room. The room that only he had a key to and could go to. The same room where he was to be disturbed when he entered it. He stood before the door and produced a key. Opening it he allowed the princess to enter first. She entered slowly and her eyes filled with tears as she looked around.

"It is the same as I remembered it" she whispered.

"Father had not let anyone in after you left, not even the maids. I followed after him."

They walked over to the bed and the princess sat down slowly. To her left on the nightstand were all of the letters that she had wrote and sent. She looked at Charles.

"I have kept them, every last one of them." he told her. He walked over and picked up a handful. "From time to time I come here and read them. I have not touched anything else here except to dust and keep the cob-webs away." he placed them back down and looked at her. "We did not believe that you had ran off. But father and I could not prove otherwise. He was heartbroken until the day he died. I, I have been lonely here ever since." he sat down next to her. "Then you sent Jared. You did not let me know where you were." he got up and walked over to the borough. "I was forced into silence. They wanted to kill your son, to hunt you down. They blamed you for all types of threats, to me. To the throne they would say." Charles went on to tell her how the nobles turned against her and then himself. His own mother and now his Queen, his wife. He told her about the council's decision on the Royal Messengers and his decision to keep Michael on to train Jared. He protected him the best he could. Georgette let him tell his story without interrupting. She watched him as he paced back and forth in front of the borough. She was reminded of him as a child coming to her and telling her of all he had discovered while eavesdropping on the servants of their father. All the mysterious things he found out. His face was always serious when he told her his stories, trying to get in all the details.

The next morning King Charles had it publicly announced that the Princess Georgette had been returned home. He declared the perpetrators and families against him and his family, and that they would be punished. He declared that the Queen Alicene had committed treason and would be put to death in three days by public hanging. Jared was declared his nephew along with George. It was already known that they were at civil war with the nobles of their own land. Lord Robert Loch of Auber Meadows, Lord Gregory of Mountainview, Lord Wilford of Vineland, and Lord Brandon of Acco. Thereafter they would set out after the kingdom of Chamell. The citizens roared with excitement at this and the next day the watched the guillotine built.

King Charles and Princess Georgette had gone to check in on Jared and George repeatedly for the next couple of days. George was recovering well, but Jared, he had only gained consciousness one and King Charles was not there then.

Lord John had returned to the castle and with him Lord Brandon, his wife and son; Lord Wilford and his two sons. They were all bound captive. It only took three days to run out Lord Brandon. Most of his men did not know of his treachery and turned on him when they found out. Lord Wilford held out for eight days. A maidservant that had just been hired by him had turned out to be a spy of King Charles. She let in Lord John's men and they took hold of the noble and his castle. Lord John had sent the rest of his men to aid Lord Jeffery. Lord Gregory and Lord Robert were still held under siege.

The two lords, Wilford and Brandon had openly admitted to their part in the scheme and argued how they felt justified. They said that King Charles., like his father before him was against the tradition of their kingdom and had not held up to their standards. They were to die with the queen. All the men of the two lords' land that Lord John thought trust worthy were to join with the king's men at the boarder of Chamell and be assigned under the leading commander there. None were to be given any rank and they were to be placed out on the front lines. Lord John would stay the night and leave in the morning with more orders.

At the evening meal the table was full of food and the seats around it were full. King Charles and Princess Georgette spoke heartily. King Gaston was there with his queen and children. Caleb sat next to Princess Elizabeth and they chatted. The two had grown close since they discovered the plot against the king and his sister, Jared as well. This evening meal almost seemed like a typical meal for the royal family. They ate and drank, talked and laughed. Even at these times of war they seemed happy.

The Royal Messenger's presence cut silence in the dining hall. On second look it was not Jared, but George that stood at the doorway. His appearance was so much like Jared's, his older brother. Only he had not that deathly stare upon his face as Jared would, however his face was serious. Serious with sorrow. His eyes were set upon the princess, his mother. He was not fully recovered, but looked a lot better than he did when he showed up to the castle a few days past. Slowly he walked over to his mother and she knew immediately what he would say. Tears streamed down her face as she began to plead no. he small hands gripped tightly his shirt.

"No, no, please no. George do not tell me. No! I've waited too long, too long to see him!" she cried. Her words were felt by everyone in the hall. George hung his head and placed a hand on her shoulder.

"I am sorry mother, he is gone. Jared is gone." he told her.

Her tears fell like waterfalls and she wailed loudly as she clinged tightly to George. King Charles jumped up out of his chair and ran out of the dining hall. His feet carried him to the medics' quarters where he burst through the doors startling everyone. He seen Jared shirtless, lifeless laid upon the bed.

"Fix him!" he yelled an order grabbing the doctor by the shirt. "Bring him back!" he shoved the doctor over to where Jared's body lay.

"Your Majesty, we have tried. Truly we have. There is nothing we can do." the doctor coward on the floor where he fell.

King Charles grabbed another man, "Bring him back!" he said through clenched teeth. "I command you."

"We have tried Your Majesty. For, for over an hour we have tried."

"For over an hour?!" the king yelled. He drew his blade from his side and would have cut the doctor down, Princess Georgette's voice stayed his hand.

"Charles! Don't do it." she said from the doorway. "He is gone. Will you kill these men unjustly?"

King Charles' rage took him and he yelled pushing over the doctor's bottles, vials, papers, and other contents from the counter. Everyone flinched not knowing where to go or what to do. He knelt down at the bedside where his nephew's body lay and sobbed. Caleb, Princess Elizabeth, and George stood at the doorway. Princess Georgette went in the room and sat on the bed next to where Charles knelt. She picked up Jared's cold hand and held it in hers.

"I am sorry my son, I am so very sorry." she said softly, her tears were all gone.

The doctors eased out of the room leaving the royal family to grieve. The time for tears and sorrow had not yet passed, King Charles would be in the same position in the morning.

After the morning meal was announced the king was told that the Princess Georgette had passed in her sleep. She lay in her bed looking peaceful and again King Charles knelt by a bedside sobbing. Hours later he walked slowly from the princess' room. Red eyed and zombie like he walked down to the dungeon where the queen and nobles were held.

"Are you satisfied?" he asked standing in front of the queen's cell door. "They are both dead. My sister and her son Jared is dead. They are no-longer a threat to the throne." he hung his head shaking it. "Does it satisfy you to hear that?"

"What we did was for you and our daughter." Queen Alicene said walking up to the cell bars. "It was done for Elizabeth's future. Nothing was to happen while you lived." she stood in front of King Charles with only the bars separating them.

"You have helped destroy my family."

"I was securing our daughters future."

"How? By taking their kingdom away from her, away from her people."

"It was for her own good and the kingdom."

"All this time as I loved you, you… you plotted against me. You betrayed. You betrayed your own daughter."

"She would have messed things up. She could not see how things would have turned out. Charles you are blind and she is just like ….huh."

His hands shot through the bars and grabbed her by the throat cutting off her words and wind. "Blind." he growled. "You turned against your own flesh and blood and you call me blind." she beat at his hands as her face began to turn red." He shoved her away and she gasped for air with her hands at her neck. "Blind? You say I am blind, I will show you exactly how blind I am" he turned and strode away. Loudly he told her and everyone in the dungeon. "I will show you all how blind I am" the dungeon door slammed loudly behind him.

At high noon outside in the square, the crowd was abuzz. Everyone was trying to get closer in to the front. They squeezed and pushed their way about in the thick crowd. Seven guillotines could be seen and guards stood about them. King Charles had sat at the end of the stage and both his daughters sat beside him. George stood behind him. There were other guest nobles present around the stage as well. The nobles were brought out then the queen. They were all lead up on the stage. None of the nobles protested but walked proudly with their eyes set on the crowd. The queen however only had eyes for the clad in black. A Royal Messenger? A man that was not Jared but resembled him greatly. How could this be she thought. All the nobles were placed under a guillotine and the guards waited for the king's orders. One by one a guillotine fell upon the king's signal, a head falling from a noble's body. A guard stood by the queen and waited his orders, it never came. King Charles got up and walked over to the Queen.

"Many battles you have secretly won," he said looking down at her. "But, did you know that there was another one? My sister, Princess Georgette; had another son. I have given him the choice to rule any land he chooses as lord under my kingdom or sit as king in your cousins' land. I will win this war, and a son of the Princess Georgette will be crowned king. By him many more Royal Messengers may be trained." the king took the rope from the guard and pulled on it. The blade fell and the queen's head fell and rolled at his feet. He looked down at it and walked away.

In the weeks that followed all of Lord Robert's men were rounded and killed. King Charles did not have time to wait out a year long siege. The river and any other water supply to each mansion was cut off. Burning pitch was catapulted over their walls and in windows. The people inside were smoked out and surrounded. Lord Robert had been found hanging in his room. His supporters were rooted out just as Lord Gregory's were and they were all put to death at once. King Charles' army grew with the soldiers of the dead Lords. These men were to be used as front men and foot soldiers. The king knew that many of them were only following their lord's orders, but still he stripped them of any rank. He did not have time to sort out who was actually loyal to him or not. He had another battle to fight. A war waged on the Chamell's. He decide to take his kingdom.

King Charles looked over at George who was fully recovered and in better shape due to Jared's notes he found in his room. Something that no Royal Messenger had ever done before. Jared had wrote down notes of his training, healing and fighting style, and had them locked away. When he passed, King Charles allowed George too have full access to his room and he had discovered them. George used some of the meditation trances and potions to heal himself faster. Now he stood by his uncle's side ready for battle.

King Charles looked over at Caleb who knew the fighting style of the Royal Messengers and was just as ready. He had taken Jared's weapons and cape as his own now.

Line upon line, rank upon rank; men stood at the boarders of Chamell and awaited the King's command. King Charles had spotted King Perciville in the opposing force that came across the land spread out just as far as his men.

"Caleb, George." the king said both of their names and the two men rode out. One to the right and the other to the left. King Charles raised his hand and as King Perciville's men advanced he let his sword fall. The two forces yelled and charged each other.

The End

Printed in the United States
By Bookmasters